A LOW MOAN ESCAPED HER LIPS . . .

as he forcefully pulled her against him, pinning her arms with his own while his mouth came down on hers. With a will of its own, her body curved to the contours of his, responding in the only possible manner to his compelling caresses. Suddenly she was caught up in an intoxicating spell she could not escape, possessed by an overwhelming desire she could no longer deny . . .

Stephanie Richards grew up in a small Midwestern town, and, as she says, "Traveling had always been a big part of my dreams." Now, as a wife and mother of two children, Richards has traveled half the United States and looks forward to seeing the other half. In addition to writing, she enjoys swimming, painting, and good music.

Dear Reader:

Signet has always been known for its consistently fine individual romances, and now we are proud to introduce a provocative new line of contemporary romances, RAPTURE ROMANCE. While maintaining our high editorial standards, RAPTURE ROMANCE will explore all the possibilities that exist when today's men and women fall in love. Mutual respect, gentle affection, raging passion, tormenting jealousy, overwhelming desire, and finally, pure rapture—the moods of romance will be vividly presented in the kind of sensual yet always tasteful detail that makes a fantasy real. We are very enthusiastic about RAPTURE ROMANCE, and we hope that you will enjoy reading these novels as much as we enjoy finding and publishing them for you!

In fact, please let us know what you do think—we love to hear from our readers, and what you tell us about your likes and dislikes is taken seriously. We have enclosed a questionnaire with some of our own queries at the back of this book. Please take a few minutes to fill it out, or if you prefer, write us directly at the address below.

And don't forget that your favorite RAPTURE ROMANCE authors need your encouragement; although we can't give out addresses, we will be happy to forward any mail.

We look forward to hearing from you!

Robin Grunder
RAPTURE ROMANCE
New American Library
1633 Broadway
New York, NY 10019

CHESAPEAKE AUTUMN

by

Stephanie Richards

PUBLISHER'S NOTE

This novel is a work of fiction. Names, characters, places, and incidents are either the product of the author's imagination or are used fictitiously, and any resemblance to actual persons, living or dead, events, or locales is entirely coincidental.

NAL BOOKS ARE AVAILABLE AT QUANTITY DISCOUNTS WHEN USED TO PROMOTE PRODUCTS OR SERVICES. FOR INFORMATION PLEASE WRITE TO PREMIUM MARKETING DIVISION, THE NEW AMERICAN LIBRARY, INC., 1633 BROADWAY, NEW YORK, NEW YORK 10019.

SIGNET, SIGNET CLASSICS, MENTOR, PLUME, MERIDIAN AND NAL BOOKS are published by The New American Library, Inc., 1633 Broadway, New York, New York 10019

First Printing, February, 1983

1 2 3 4 5 6 7 8 9

PRINTED IN THE UNITED STATES OF AMERICA

Chapter One

Leaning into the wind, Deirdre Logan brought the *Jessy Bess* around, heading for the cove and home. Warm, summerlike breezes had filled the sail that day, but now, with the setting sun turning the coastline into a ribbon of fiery reds and golds, there was no doubt left in Deirdre's mind that autumn had finally arrived. In a few weeks the air would be crisp and the sky would fill with hundreds of thousands of Canadian geese making their way to the tidewaters to spend the winter months. For now, Deirdre gave herself to the tranquillity of the scene before her and sailed toward the bottleneck cove that dipped inland as though it were a secret hideaway.

Even though the day had been glorious, Deirdre's thoughts hadn't been far from Andy, her son. A respite from his sickbed had been just what she had needed, but it didn't seem right somehow—enjoying a complete day of freedom while he was stuck in bed with a virus and only Craig to keep him entertained. It was particularly hard because Deirdre knew how much Andy loved to sail with her. Even at three years old he showed all the signs of being a true Mallory in that respect. He might be the image of his father, but that had no bearing on it at all, Deirdre decided firmly, giving in to a twinge of resentment. She hadn't felt the emotion in a very long time and she checked it instantly, refusing to dwell on a past that could not be changed and concentrating instead on the contentment she had found building a life alone for her and her son.

The Chesapeake itself was part of that contentment, Deirdre acknowledged. Aware of the magnificence of her surroundings, she was at the same time oblivious of the contribution she herself made to the picturesque setting. The sunset was pure gold, dancing off the water and capturing the burnished copper of Deirdre's hair as it swung freely down her back. Her sparkling emerald-green eyes took everything in at a glance, but at no time in her twenty-seven years had Deirdre ever taken this vast beauty for granted.

Riding the waves raised by a fishing trawler in the distance, Deirdre prepared to berth the sailboat alongside the other craft using the Mallorys' private dock. Most of the owners were weekenders who would have already started the long drive back to Washington, leaving their boats in the care of their trusted friend, Craig Mallory, for yet another week. For the past few years this had been an adequate source of income for her young cousin, and for this, Deirdre was grateful. Living with Craig after the accident—which had left him partially crippled and scarred both physically and emotionally—had been difficult at best. Working on the boats kept Craig's hands and mind occupied, thus enabling their lives to run much more smoothly.

Deirdre was bringing in the sail when she spied the lone man striding toward the dock. Even though he was some distance away, Deirdre recognized Roy Carlysle's familiar walk and the blond lightness of his sun-bleached hair, which emphasized a somewhat boyish attractiveness in the thirty-seven-year-old attorney.

They had been friends for four years now, Deirdre thought pensively. Roy had walked into her life the day Garth Logan had walked out of it, and, although Deirdre knew Roy had been sent by Garth to "look after her" in those long months following Craig's accident, she had found his gentle kindness and easy charm a welcome distraction from the harsh realities that had suddenly taken over her life. In those early weeks Deirdre had been like a child lost in a storm. She would have relied heavily on Roy if he had allowed it, but instead he had made her aware of her own strength, her own capabilities.

But that all seemed a very long time ago. Something had happened to the easy rapport they had once shared. The change had been so subtle, Deirdre hadn't realized Roy was becoming attracted to her until it was too late to stop it without hurting him. Deirdre had never knowingly encouraged Roy beyond the bounds of friendship, nor had she wanted to. Roy was a married man and she, for all purposes, was a married woman. Even in her wildest imaginings Deirdre could not see herself as a homewrecker.

She was tying up the *Jessy Bess* when Roy reached the dock. She hadn't seen him in several days, even though he kept an apartment in town despite the fact that his thriving law practice was located in Baltimore. Roy handled all her legal affairs, including taxes and her investments, which the successful boutique she owned locally allowed her to make. But, intuitively, she knew it wasn't a business matter that brought him to see her now.

"Have you been waiting long?" she asked, securing the boat before standing to face him.

Roy eyed her appreciatively, making Deirdre fully aware of her knit shorts and the thin strapped top that clung to her body. The scrawniness of girlhood had long ago given way to generous curves at her hips and waist, taut yet shapely thighs, and firm, beautifully formed breasts acquired through motherhood. A day spent in the autumn sunshine did nothing to detract from her healthy appearance, but rather than be pleased by this, Deirdre felt ridiculously uncomfortable under Roy's gaze.

"I've been hanging around awhile," Roy admitted a bit shyly, hooking his thumbs into the pockets of his jeans. He had been legally separated from his wife for three months now, but the white mark on the third finger of his left hand was as much a brand as any wedding ring could be.

"I didn't mean to stay out so long," Deirdre said, raking her sun-browned hands through her wind-tossed hair.

"I'm glad you took the boat out, Deirdre. You won't have many weekends like this left for sailing. I'm surprised it's stayed warm this late, aren't you?"

Deirdre nodded but failed to comment. Idle chatter wasn't a strong point between them, and she knew Roy hadn't come to discuss the unseasonably warm weather.

"Why don't you help me check the buckets for crabs while you tell me what's on your mind," she prompted with an encouraging smile. She turned and walked to the end of the dock, leaving Roy to bring the net from the boat. But she got no further than lifting the buckets from the water before Roy stopped her.

"Deirdre, let that go for a minute. I have something . . . important to tell you."

From her kneeling position, Deirdre turned to face him. "You sound rather grim," she mused. "What happened? Did the market close down today?"

Instead of smiling, Roy sighed heavily. "I wish that was all. It's Garth, Deirdre. He's back in town."

Deirdre felt as if she were suddenly carved from stone. It had taken her quite some time to accept the fact that she had a husband she didn't know any better than some stranger on the street, but once she had, she had been able to pick up the pieces of her life. She had made a fresh start on her own, because her husband couldn't care less if he ever got to know her or their son. If Garth cared about anyone, it was only Jasamin Grant, the girl Deirdre would always blame for so recklessly touching their lives and leaving behind nothing but pain and destruction. But proving Garth's devotion to Jasamin wouldn't help . . . nor would it make Craig any less bitter, she acknowledged ruefully, checking her unproductive thoughts.

"What does he want?" she asked with surprising calm.

Roy shrugged. "I'm not sure. I only spoke with him for a few minutes on the telephone. I had no idea he was coming here. He says he wants to meet with me in the morning." Deirdre could tell by the tone of his voice that Roy wasn't pleased by this, but for the life of her she couldn't imagine why. After all, Roy and Garth were best friends. At least, that was what she had always believed.

"He must be here on business, then," she surmised, turning back to the task at hand with an air of nonchalance. Garth was back in town. Just like that! After four years she could hardly get excited about the idea. Disturbed, yes. Excited, never!

"I imagine that's part of it," Roy said, bringing the net over to help her with the catch. Deirdre's hand froze when he added, "He intends to see you and the boy, Deirdre. He made that quite clear."

A spark of pride ignited deep inside her. Drawing a deep breath, she said, "So let him. As long as he keeps paying the bills, I really don't care what he does."

It was a brave statement, but, in truth, Garth Logan was the last person Deirdre wanted to see. Roy had acted as liaison between them for four years now, and that was precisely the way she wanted things to continue.

Ironic that Garth should show up now, Deirdre thought, just when his son was becoming old enough to be curious about his father. For Andy's sake, Deirdre had always painted a grand and glorious picture of Garth, stressing the importance of his work in Central America. A child Andy's age couldn't rationally understand that his father placed his wife and child second in his life and always would. He only knew his father was an important man and worked for the government. At least that knowledge placed Andy in an enviable position with his friends, who had normal daddies who did mundane things like come home every night. How long Andy would remain happy about his father's uniqueness, Deirdre had no way of knowing.

Deirdre dragged a hand over her pounding temple. "Did you mention this to Craig?" she asked.

"No. I thought you should know first. To be honest, I wasn't sure how Craig would react to the news. I was hoping, for your sake, that he would have come to terms with it by now."

Deirdre shook her head, recalling the contempt in Craig's eyes the day she had told him that she was carrying Garth Logan's child and that he had agreed to marry her. She hadn't realized until then how deeply he hated Garth.

"Craig can be very stubborn when he wants to be," Deirdre said, thinking of how unreasonable his hatred for Garth was. "It amazes me sometimes how loving and gentle he can be with Andy when his resentment for Andy's father is so deep. It's as though he blames Garth for the accident," she concluded with a shake of her head.

"But that's ridiculous, Deirdre. Garth had nothing to do with it. He wasn't even there."

"I know," she said resolutely. "But Garth is 'connected' to Jasamin Grant, and she *was* there. How can Craig possibly come to terms with it all when he can't even bring himself to mention the girl's name?"

"Maybe you should warn Craig about Garth's being here," Roy suggested.

"Yes, I'll find a way to tell him. Where is Garth staying?" she asked, wondering just how much Roy actually knew about this unexpected visit. He looked far too uneasy to be as uninformed as he pretended to be.

"He's in town, at the Bayview. At least, that's where he's registered. I, uh . . . did some checking," he admitted uncomfortably.

"I see." Deirdre lowered her eyes. Business first, she added silently, wondering why she'd even bothered to ask. Pushing the thought aside, she turned to meet Roy's blue eyes questioningly. "You don't seem very pleased about his being here."

She regretted doubting him the moment he said, "I just don't want it all dredged up for you again, Deirdre. I don't think I could stand seeing you hurt again."

Deirdre compressed her lips tightly. "You needn't worry about me. I'm not as vulnerable as I once was."

She forced her lips to curve into a smile. "Now, if you want some dinner, you'd better help me with these crabs."

Roy laughed and opened the net as Deirdre, armed with long clamps, took four large crabs from the buckets. She had gotten pinched once too often not to have learned her lesson.

The yield of blue crabs from the estuary hadn't been that plentiful in recent years, but Mr. Hicks never failed to leave them a sampling of his catch each week. He claimed it was a fair exchange, since Craig fixed his old furnace every winter. Deirdre was certain Mr. Hicks was coming out short on the deal, but she'd never convince him of that. When she saw crabs like these, she was glad she couldn't.

Roy didn't stay for dinner, but he rarely did unless they had business to discuss. Instead he walked her to the back door of her two-story farmhouse and promised to be nearby if she needed him. But Deirdre knew she wouldn't. Her vulnerability had been replaced by an inner strength long ago, when her son was born and she realized how very much he needed her. For Andy she would do anything—she could survive anything—including seeing the man she had married by proxy four years earlier.

Deirdre deposited the crabs in a saltwater container off the back porch before entering the house. The Mallory homestead had been around for five generations and judging by its size and sturdiness, it would be around for many more. The clapboard siding was familiar to the area, but the three distinguishable roofs, a result of expansion over the years, were a unique sight indeed.

The kitchen was filled with inviting odors that warmed Deirdre to the core of her being. She entered just as Edith Kirk was getting ready to leave for the day.

Edith was priceless, caring for Andy during the week while Deirdre worked at the boutique and Craig attended to the boats that needed servicing. Deirdre had been flippant about Garth paying the bills, but in truth, the only expenses she would allow him to cover were those pertaining to Craig's medical bills, which were exorbitant. Aside from that, she and Craig managed a comfortable living that satisfied their simple tastes and needs. Being married to a man who was quite wealthy by her own standards mattered little to Deirdre. She had never felt comfortable enough in her role as his wife to ask for any luxuries from him. It was just as well she didn't have to.

"I didn't expect you to stay so late, Edith," Deirdre commented apologetically.

The plumpish woman flipped a hand at her. "I don't have anything better to do at home anyway. Fact is, I'm getting worried about that boy of yours and I wanted to stay and talk to you about him."

"Andy isn't worse today, is he?" she asked, instantly concerned. Andy had never been an exceptionally strong child, but Deirdre had learned to take most things concerning him in her stride. Their old family doctor had checked him over and assured her that he merely had a cold that would run its course. His fever had been intermittent, but when she left that morning there had been no sign of it. In fact, she had every reason to believe the worst was over.

"Can't say he's worse, but he sure isn't getting any better. Doc Foggarty is a good man, but he isn't a pediatrician. I want you to promise me you'll have young Andy checked over by someone else."

Deirdre didn't want to stand there arguing about Dr. Foggarty's abilities. Andy adored the man, and Deirdre had always felt comfortable with him as well. She'd never really considered a second opinion necessary, but now . . .

"I'll call for an appointment on Monday, Edith," she promised, knowing the woman would have never made such a suggestion unless she felt it was absolutely necessary. "Are those cinnamon rolls I smell?" Deirdre asked, hoping to shift the woman's thoughts to a more appealing topic.

"Fresh from the oven." Edith beamed, momentarily distracted. She turned to collect her things and added,

"Now, you heed my warning. I've got a feeling something is seriously wrong with that boy."

The door closed with a quiet click but Deirdre jerked as if it had been slammed soundly. Edith Kirk wasn't one to overdramatize a situation. Deirdre had gotten used to her stories about raising six kids through every ailment imaginable, but she couldn't ignore the anxiety she felt over her own son.

Deirdre climbed the stairs to the second-story landing. She paused only a moment outside Andy's bedroom door, listening to the story Craig was reading to him. It was *Goldilocks and the Three Bears,* Andy's favorite, although at one time it had given him terrifying nightmares. Craig had a graphic way with children's stories.

"Can I come in?" Deirdre asked, peeking in from outside the door.

"It's 'may I,' Mommy," Andy informed her smartly, reminding her of the zillion times she'd corrected him for the same error.

"Watch it, kid," she threatened playfully. "I'm the mom and you're the kid. Remember that, will you?"

Andy giggled as Deirdre sat on the edge of the bed and quickly brought her hand to his forehead. It was warm again and she sighed with frustration.

"Feeling better, darling?" she asked.

He looked up at her with the dark, shiny eyes he had inherited from his father. "A little bit, I guess. I wish I could have gone sailing with you. I'll bet I would have been all well by now if I had."

"Mmm, you could be right," she said, casting a knowing smile at Craig. "Next time, okay?"

He turned up his nose. "My tummy feels hot inside," Andy complained.

Accustomed to such maneuvering, Deirdre smiled. "And I'll just bet some strawberry ice cream would cool it off. Right?"

To her surprise, Andy shook his head. "I don't think so, Mommy."

Deirdre shot Craig a concerned look, but he merely shrugged. "Get some sleep, sport," Craig told him gently. "You'll feel better in the morning."

Those parting words had become commonplace. Hearing them yet again, Deirdre wondered just how much she'd taken for granted as far as her son's health was concerned.

The pine stairs creaked as Deirdre and Craig walked down side by side. Once out of Andy's earshot, Deirdre said, "Edith thinks I should take him to another doctor. A specialist."

Craig lifted a hand to massage his stiff shoulder. "You know what a worrier Edith can be sometimes. Andy's like one of her grandkids."

Craig's lack of concern was indicative of his attitude toward just about everything, Deirdre thought sadly. It wasn't that he didn't care for Andy; it was just that Craig had never been the sort to borrow trouble. Knowing this, Deirdre wondered how trouble always managed to find Craig.

They went into the kitchen and while Deirdre put on the crab boil for a salad, Craig dug into the freshly baked cinnamon rolls. As he walked back to the table with a glass of milk in his hand, Deirdre surveyed him. He had made a miraculous recovery after the car crash, even though initially the doctors hadn't thought he would survive. Paralysis seemed a foregone conclusion in the weeks that followed, but Craig proved to have a stronger will than anyone had credited him with. Exactly ten months after the accident, he took his first step alone. Now, aside from the scars he bore, the only physical evidence remaining was a limp, which was bad only during the inactive cold-weather months, and the almost imperceptible fact that his left shoulder was lower than his right. Even Deirdre noticed only because Craig favored his left shoulder, as if protecting it from further harm.

The accident had been devastating for Craig. He had the Mallory dark and mysterious good looks, which had brought him the attentions of more than a fair share of girls. Looking at him now, Deirdre had trouble even remembering the carefree youth he had once been. At twenty-two, he seemed years older than Deirdre herself.

Craig had come to live with Deirdre and her father after his own parents had died in a fire that, tragically, he had witnessed. He was barely ten years old then, and Deirdre, five years his senior, had become his big sister. Three years later, her father died unexpectedly, leaving an eighteen-year-old Deirdre to care for her young cousin. She vowed to keep him with her. Together they fought every agency in the county and, with the help of good friends like Edith Kirk and Mr. Hicks, they won.

Many times over the years, Deirdre had questioned that decision, wondering how different things might have been, particularly for Craig, if she had let him go. But at the time it had seemed so right that they should stay together. They had no one else, and Deirdre was more than willing to take on the responsibility. Willing, and capable. Her mother had been a semiinvalid until her death shortly before Craig came to live with them, and she had taught Deirdre how to run a home efficiently. Deirdre fell back on that training during the years she and Craig were alone.

"Lover Boy was hanging around again," Craig said, cutting into her thoughts sharply.

Deirdre sighed, knowing he meant Roy. Craig never pretended to like Roy, but he failed to provide her with an explanation for his dislike that made sense. As far as Craig was concerned, Roy was part of a chain that led back to Jasamin and Garth, and that was reason enough. How did one even begin to argue with that sort of logic? she wondered.

"You know Roy and I are not romantically involved," she said, wishing she could laugh away such childish remarks. But in order to maintain a level of stability in their lives, Deirdre had learned to cater to Craig's moods for the most part.

Craig smiled sardonically. "Not for lack of trying, I dare say. On his part, at least."

Deirdre frowned disapprovingly. "Roy and Olivia are having some problems, but I think they're trying to work things out."

Craig chuckled softly. "If he is, he has a strange way of going about it. He'd divorce her in a minute if he thought he stood a chance of getting you into bed."

Deirdre's eyes widened at his boldness. Usually Deirdre went out of her way to avoid an argument with Craig, but this time she had more on her mind than she could easily deal with. The knowledge that Garth was in town left her more on edge than she realized.

"I don't deserve that, Craig. And, for that matter, neither does Roy," she blurted out sharply.

Her outburst surprised Craig, but his reaction left Deirdre even more puzzled than he was. Craig was an enigma to her. He could be so gentle and caring one minute, so provoking the next. It was as if it was all a game to him. Ambivalence dictated their relationship and Deirdre longed for the days before the accident, when they had been so content.

"Sorry, Dee," Craig muttered, reaching for another hot roll. She wondered if he had bothered to eat a decent meal in days. "I was only kidding anyway."

Deirdre looked at him and shook her head. "You drive me nuts sometimes, Craig," she said with a laugh.

Her laughter died when Craig asked suddenly, "So what did Lover Boy want, anyway?"

So much for breaking the news gently, she thought, sighing with frustration. "Roy wanted me to know Garth was back in Washington. On business, I suppose."

Craig looked at her skeptically. He knew her too well to believe that was all. "Is he coming here?"

After a moment Deirdre nodded. "He has reservations at the Bayview. I doubt he'll be staying long. Perhaps he feels it's his duty to meet his son," she said, but her attempt at cynical humor fell drastically short of its mark.

Craig was concerned about only one thing. "Is he alone?" That question had been lurking in the back of Deirdre's own mind ever since Roy had told her Garth was back. But, unlike Craig, she hadn't asked, simply because she didn't want to hear the answer.

"I don't know, Craig. Roy didn't mention Jasamin being with him." She paused, then said, "I really doubt he would bring her back here, don't you?"

"How the hell am I supposed to know what he'd do?" Craig barked, pushing himself away from the table. "I'm going to bed," he announced, striding from the room.

"Craig, wait!" Deirdre cried, but he was already gone, and she hadn't the will to go after him. Not this time. She had enough to do in dealing with her own mixed emotions over Garth's return. Craig would have to deal with his own as well.

Rising from the table, Deirdre walked over to the stove and turned it off. A meal no longer interested her. Instead she fixed a pot of herb tea and carried it, along with a newly arrived magazine, into the living room.

The simplicity of the room struck her. Nothing in it had really changed over the years. The furnishings were durable and although the green brocade on the sofa had worn with age, it still had a few more years in it.

Pouring a cup of tea, Deirdre settled onto the end of the sofa. Leaving the magazine untouched on the coffee table, she blew lightly on the tea to cool it, and let her thoughts wander back to the point in her life when her well-ordered existence had begun to change.

Chapter Two

It wasn't accurate to say the change had begun the day she met Garth Logan. More precisely, it had begun with the termination of her engagement to Steven Blake. She had known Steven almost all her life. She dated him all through high school, graduating the same year he finished college. Everyone agreed that they should wait until after Steven finished medical school to be married, but their engagement became official two months prior to her father's death. Becoming lovers had also seemed part of the natural order of things and while sex with Steven hadn't been the earthshaking experience she had expected, it didn't diminish her love for Steven or her desire to become his wife.

Everything changed shortly after her father's death, when Steven decided they would alter their plans and be married right away. Her love went out like a light as soon as he said, "The problem will be finding someone to take Craig off our hands." That was the last she saw of Steven Blake.

It was several months before Deirdre began dating again, but the thought of having an intimate relationship with any of the men she dated left her cold. But that was before she met Garth.

From the moment she opened the door to him that spring afternoon, she was irresistibly drawn to him. There was an aura about him, she noticed, that went beyond mere good looks. There was strength in that handsomely chiseled face—character, her father would have called it.

Sharp, intelligent eyes surveyed her as thoroughly as she surveyed him, but if he was put off by such aggressiveness in a woman, he didn't let it show. Instead, he seemed almost pleased by the way she met his gaze. No doubt he was more accustomed to delicate-looking beauties, swooning at his feet.

The very thought made Deirdre take stock of her own appearance. Dressed in snug-fitting jeans and a shirt of Craig's that hit her mid-thigh, she looked neither delicate nor likely to swoon. What she looked was busy, which was precisely what she had been before he had rung the bell and dragged her away from the rigorous task of spring cleaning. Nevertheless, Deirdre made an attempt to look presentable by tugging the triangle scarf from her head, leaving her copper-colored hair tumbling down around her shoulders. Stripped of makeup, her green eyes flashed brilliantly behind long, silken lashes. When, upon seeing her, the stranger's interest was suddenly piqued, Deirdre smiled.

"May I help you?" she asked, being the first to break the lingering silence.

"That depends," he said rather sharply. "I was told Craig Mallory lives here. You are his cousin, Deirdre, I presume."

Deirdre could only marvel at the transformation of his features when he spoke of Craig, his obvious reason for being there. His tobacco-brown hair was swept back off his forehead in a gesture of impatience. The warmth previously emanating from those dark eyes had faded and in its place was steely determination. Finally, his jawline had taken on a rugged look, and his compressed lips hid the sensual fullness of his mouth.

"I'm Deirdre Mallory," she acknowledged. "I'm sorry, but Craig isn't home right now. Was he expecting you?" she asked, noting the tired lines that appeared around his eyes and mouth.

"I seriously doubt it." His tone was dry as he stepped inside. Instinctively Deirdre backed farther into the foyer, feeling suddenly closed in by his towering presence. "I'm looking for your cousin, Miss Mallory, because I have every reason to believe he and my ward, Jasamin Grant, have run off this weekend to be married."

Deirdre stared incredulously, resisting the urge to laugh. They couldn't possibly be talking about the same Craig Mallory. Not *her* Craig Mallory!

"I'm sorry, but you've obviously made some sort of mistake. You say this girl is your ward?" She had never heard the name before and she knew all of Craig's friends.

"That's right. My name is Garth Logan. Jasamin attends a girl's boarding school in Baltimore. She's been seeing your cousin for several months now, and last night . . ."

Deirdre began shaking her head, certain that he had the wrong person. "As I said, Mr. Logan, you've made a mistake. Craig doesn't keep secrets from me, and I can assure you, I've never heard the girl's name before. Besides, Craig is on a weekend fishing trip with friends from school."

Garth Logan's eyes lowered over her slowly, taking in any detail he might have missed earlier. Satisfied, he brought his eyes back to meet hers. "You can't be that naive, Miss Mallory. I doubt very seriously your eighteen-year-old cousin tells you *all* of his secrets."

Deirdre moistened her lips, her eyes never wavering from his. If his intention was to make her doubt Craig, he couldn't have chosen a more provocative way to do it.

"Craig isn't the sort to run off with anyone," she persisted, but even she could hear the conviction faltering in her tone. "You have to understand, Mr. Logan, Craig and I are very close. If he was seeing this girl, he would have told me about her."

Garth drew a deep breath. Clearly his patience was wearing thin. From the welt pocket of his shirt he extracted a picture and handed it to her. Deirdre stared in disbelief. The young man in the picture was definitely Craig, and the girl he had his arms laced around so possessively was clearly no stranger. Long blond hair hung over one shoulder to her waist, and all Deirdre could think of was how remarkably beautiful the girl was for one so very young.

"She's very pretty," Deirdre muttered. "But that picture hardly proves . . ."

Her words died when, from the same pocket, he extracted a piece of paper, and promptly handed it to her. Deirdre unfolded it and read silently:

> Garth:
>
> I've had enough of your domineering attitude. I'm going away so you'll never see me again. As for my inheritance, Daddy's will stated that I would receive the bulk of the estate upon my marriage, should I marry before my twenty-first birthday. Whatever drastic measures I might take, be assured you drove me to it.
>
> JASAMIN

"This photograph and note were the only things left in Jasamin's room at school," Garth explained. "They called me last night and told me Jasamin had run away. I caught an early flight and arrived just a while ago. Now I'm damn tired, Miss Mallory, so I'm only going to say this once. I know my ward. Leaving this picture behind was no accident—certainly not with the boy's name and address clearly printed on the back."

Deirdre bit the soft flesh of her lower lip. She didn't like the sharpness of his tone, but if what he said was true, he certainly had a right to be testy. She hadn't been easy to convince.

"In other words, she wants you to find her," said Deirdre, handing the note back to him.

"Very astute, Miss Mallory."

Deirdre drew a breath for patience. "Then she'll undoubtedly come back on her own, and I would venture to say she'll come back unmarried. She doesn't sound exactly stupid."

Garth's mouth twisted into a sneer. "Let's just hope your cousin is as smart. Jasamin is seventeen years old, a minor in the eyes of the law. If he touches her, or if he's crossed the state line with her, I'll have him brought up on charges so fast he won't know what hit him."

Deirdre gasped at his threat. "Now, just a minute! From the sound of that note this flower of yours is hardly an innocent lamb!"

Garth's jaw hardened. "Whether she is or isn't is none of your concern . . . yet! Now, do you help me find her or shall we wait it out hoping they'll get cold feet at the altar?"

If Deirdre hadn't felt certain that he would follow through with his threat, she would have ordered him from her house. His authoritative manner was enough to make her rebel out of stubbornness alone.

As it was, she had no choice but to lead the way upstairs to Craig's room, where they began a systematic search of his personal belongings. What Garth Logan hoped to find, she didn't know. She couldn't imagine Craig leaving a note as the girl had done. But, then she couldn't imagine Craig pulling a stunt like this in the first place.

"You want to tell me what we're looking for?" Deirdre asked, sorting through a dresser drawer that looked just like any drawer should look.

Garth had opened the closet door and was searching through jacket pockets and such. "Anything that might give us a clue as to where they might have gone. A friend's apartment . . . maybe even a motel."

Deirdre turned and looked at him. "Craig would never take a girl to a motel!" She sounded indignant, but her words alone were enough to elicit a doubting frown.

"My dear Miss Mallory, I think I've had a bit more experience concerning the sex habits of an eighteen-year-old male than you have."

"But you don't know Craig," she argued stiffly. "He's not . . . well, he's not typical. He's a very special young man. He even worked to pay for his own car," she declared haughtily.

Garth laughed at her tone of voice. "Sounds like a regular boy next door. Forgive me, Deirdre, but that won't get him any stars in my book."

Knowing she was gaining no ground with him, Deirdre turned back to search the drawer further.

"What's this?" Garth asked, taking a box down from the top of the closet.

Deirdre shrugged nonchalantly. "Oh, that's just some things Craig's been keeping. Personal things," she concluded, not thinking for a moment he would actually go through it.

"Mr. Logan!" she cried, following him to the bed, where he had placed the box. "I just told you those things are personal!" she insisted, but he ignored her and started to remove the lid. Deirdre's hand met the top, slamming the box closed, much to Garth Logan's surprise. "I won't allow this, Mr. Logan. You're going too far."

Garth breathed heavily, then circled her wrist with a viselike grip. "I don't have time to play games with you, Deirdre. If this shocks your principles, I'm sorry, but I intend to see what is in this box."

Her wrist hurt from the tightness of his grip, but she refused to back down. "Please," she said, hoping to appeal to his sense of decency, "you have no right."

His eyes softened for a moment, but all he said was, "Finding my ward has to be my main consideration, Deirdre. I'm sorry."

Deirdre lowered her eyes and said stiffly, "You're hurting my arm."

His grip loosened, but he didn't let her go completely. Instead he began to massage the reddened flesh.

"I didn't mean to be so rough. I'm sorry."

Deirdre pulled her arm free then, aware of the rapid beat of her pulse. She hoped he hadn't noticed the disturbing effect he had on her, but, judging by the intent way he was looking at her, she suspected he had.

She returned immediately to the dresser, leaving him to do what he felt was necessary. To her utmost surprise, he returned the box to the shelf in the closet without examining the contents after all. He gave her no explanation for his actions, but none was necessary. Garth came to stand beside her and their eyes met in the mirror above the dresser for an immeasurable length of time. I like you, Garth Logan, she thought as the corners of her mouth lifted in a soft smile. I like you very much.

"Thanks, Mr. Logan," she said aloud.

Garth shook his head and Deirdre's smile faded as she misinterpreted the gesture. "Too formal," he said. "Try Garth."

Deirdre smiled again. "Garth," she said, liking the feel of it on her tongue and the sultry way her voice made it sound.

Too soon to please Deirdre, Garth's attention was returning to the task at hand. He's out of my league anyway, Deirdre thought, taking the few extra moments allotted to stare unobserved. He looked far too sophisticated to be attracted to the daughter of a schoolteacher or the granddaughter of a fisherman. Society women were more his type, she decided firmly. Besides, the only reason you're attracted to him is that you've never met a man like Garth Logan before, Deirdre told herself. Even if he did kiss you, which he most probably would not, you'd undoubtedly find him as disappointing as all the others you go out with. As a lover he's probably better than average, but undoubtedly his experience is vast in that department.

"Now we're getting somewhere!" Garth said happily, abruptly breaking into her thoughts. He dropped his arm around her shoulder and squeezed it soundly, as if she'd discovered the small black book of personal phone numbers herself. He handed it to her, saying, "Look through these names and start making phone calls to the people you think Craig might confide in. Start with the guys.

Boys Craig's age don't generally confide in girls," he informed her knowingly.

Deirdre didn't ask how he would know such a thing. Doubtless he would remind her that he had been eighteen once himself. But somehow she couldn't imagine Garth Logan being anything like Craig at eighteen. She couldn't imagine Garth being any less confident, or any less male, than he was at that very moment.

Deirdre was still on the phone some minutes later when Garth came into the room carrying two cups of coffee. She didn't complain about his making himself at home, as the coffee was just what she needed.

"What have you found out?" Garth asked, settling quite casually beside her on the bed. Deirdre sat Indian fashion in the center of the bed with the telephone in front of her.

"His best friend's little brother finally admitted that Craig didn't go on the fishing trip, but he doesn't know where Craig did go."

Garth sighed and rubbed his neck wearily. "Keep trying, Deirdre. At this point, Craig's friends might be our only hope of finding them this evening."

Deirdre hadn't realized until then how late it was getting. Garth had arrived over an hour ago and his frustration was beginning to show.

"You must have some idea of where he might have taken her," Garth insisted. "Try to think," he urged. "You know Craig! Where would he take someone he wanted to be alone with? A place where they wouldn't be likely to be found."

Deirdre began to shake her head, then suddenly it hit her. "The cabin! My God, the island!" she screeched, feeling like a complete idiot for not thinking of it sooner. Then she realized why it had slipped her mind and she began shaking her head again. "It's been years since I've been there," she told him discouragingly. "To be honest, I don't even know if Craig still has the cabin. It belonged to his father," she explained. "Before he died, he and

Craig used to spend a lot of time there. Craig loved that place, but . . . it's been years."

Garth was off the bed instantly. "It's worth a shot, Deirdre. How do we get there?"

"We don't!" Deirdre informed him with wide-eyed incredulity. "I mean, it's not an island exactly. It's a stretch of peninsula on the eastern shore of the bay. It's accessible only by water," she concluded, "and *that* is impossible!"

"Why?" Garth frowned. "You have a boat, don't you?"

"Well, yes, of course! But it's a sailboat. In case you haven't noticed, there's a storm moving in. We'd capsize for sure."

She was throwing obstacles in his way faster than he could knock them down and she knew how annoyed he was becoming. She felt it herself and could have cried with frustration.

Chewing on her lower lip, Deirdre said, "If you wanted to risk the storm, I could borrow my friend's speedboat," she suggested as an alternative, regretting the impulsive words as soon as they were out. She'd been taught at an early age that a good sailor respects the elements and doesn't tempt fate unless he has to. She was worried about Craig, or, more importantly, what Garth might do if and when he caught up with him, but she wasn't foolish enough to court danger when it could be avoided.

Or was she, Deirdre wondered, sensing the unyielding attitude that would take Garth out in this weather no matter what the risk. She wondered fleetingly why Jasamin Grant was so special, why she warranted this kind of insanity.

"I'll ask my friend for the boat," Deirdre said with a sigh before slipping past Garth into the hallway. "Let's go."

The bay waters were choppy, half from the previous night's spring tempest and half from the storm front moving in up the coastline. Deirdre had been indifferent to it most of the day, listening to the weather reports only out of habit. Craig and his fishing friends knew enough to take shelter and that was all she was concerned about. How long ago that seemed, Deirdre thought ruefully.

Clearly Deirdre had underestimated Garth's boating experience. He made her fully aware of it when he took over the wheel of the speedboat, without even asking if she preferred to steer. She didn't object, but was sorry she hadn't when she realized the idleness gave her the unwanted opportunity to study the stranger who held her life in his hands as the boat raced over the choppy water.

He hadn't weathered the winter in any snowy region of the country. Of that she was certain. His face and hands were deeply tanned, adding to his compelling attractiveness. The name Logan was Scottish, but Deirdre had always thought of Scots as being medium to fair in coloring. Garth's stormy good looks belied that notion completely. Deirdre watched as the wind whipped the dark, tobacco-brown hair from his forehead. When his eyes narrowed against the wind, he appeared to have taken on the power of the pending storm itself.

"You realize we might not be able to make it back tonight," Deirdre said as the dark clouds moved ominously overhead. She didn't realize how easily he could have misunderstood such a remark until he looked over at her and smiled. But if his thoughts were even remotely concerned with the two of them being forced to spend the night together, he covered it well.

"It won't matter, so long as you're right about them going to the cabin. I wouldn't mind making that kid squirm all night."

Deirdre frowned disapprovingly. "You're being unreasonable, you know. It isn't fair to blame Craig for all of this."

Garth laughed pleasantly. "You're so quick to defend Craig, no matter how much proof stacks up against him. But for the record, I didn't happen to mean Craig this time."

Duly humbled, Deirdre looked away and Garth laughed

at her embarrassment. It was a strange laugh, filled with a rich, warm quality that made her feel recklessly aware of him. He was the sort she could feel comfortable with just sitting, talking . . . and laughing.

The fact that she was able to laugh at herself forced Garth to relax as well, and for a short while Deirdre felt she was seeing a side of him rarely shown to others, particularly strangers. But somehow she didn't feel that she and Garth were strangers, and she wondered just when they had crossed that boundary. Perhaps it was when she began to realize the seriousness of the situation. It was clear he cared as much for his troublesome ward as she did for her young and sometimes irresponsible cousin.

"How did you acquire the flower?" Deirdre asked, finding she wanted to know more about him, even though she knew he would walk out of her life as swiftly and as surely as he had walked into it.

Garth laughed softly. "Not by choice, I can assure you. It's rather complicated. Jasamin was the only child of my ex-wife's half-brother. Dr. Sidney Grant. You may have heard of him."

Deirdre didn't miss his casual reference to his ex-wife. Not *wife,* but ex-wife.

"Yes, I've heard of Sidney Grant. He was a Nobel scientist, wasn't he?"

Garth was clearly impressed by her knowledge. "Yes, he was. He died six months ago and he made Jasamin my ward. I also control her inheritance to a degree. It was true what she said in the note—about inheriting should she marry—but there are certain conditions."

"Conditions?"

"I have to approve of her choice of a husband," he admitted smugly.

Deirdre bristled. "Craig isn't a fortune hunter, if that's what you're thinking. We get along quite comfortably."

"I wasn't suggesting he was, or that you didn't," Garth returned dryly. "Nevertheless, I'm not going to let him marry her under any circumstances."

"What if they're already married?"

"Annulment," he stated flatly.

"And if the marriage has been consummated?" she dared suggest.

Garth shot her a menacing look that checked her taunting grin. "Then your young cousin will pay dearly," he said grimly.

Deirdre settled back in her seat, knowing they weren't far from the island. She was leery of what they might discover once they arrived there. She was nervous about what they might walk in on, but there was one thought that plagued her even more. What if this was a wild-goose chase? What if she and Garth were forced to abandon their search for the night? Could she survive the emotionally disturbing effect this man was having on her for an entire night, or was she destined to make a complete fool out of herself, knowing full well they were entirely unsuited?

The latter seemed most likely as she persisted in learning more about him. "You're not married, then." Garth shot her a strange look and she elucidated. "You mentioned your ex-wife. I assume that means you're divorced."

A smile curved his very attractive mouth. "Yes, I'm divorced and have been for several years now. I'm thirty-three and I work for the federal government as a labor lawyer, currently based in Central America," he went on, thoroughly amused. "Let's see, now . . . what else would you like to know? Oh, yes, I sleep in pajama trousers in a king-sized bed, generally alone. Does that cover everything, Deirdre?"

She glared menacingly at him but his eyes were riveted to the stretch of peninsula ahead. "That just about covers it," she mused, then added, "You're incredibly arrogant, Mr. Logan. But I doubt I'm the first woman to tell you that."

He laughed richly. "And you're very direct when you choose to be. I like that, Deirdre. I like that very much."

Her lashes fluttered at the first truly personal remark he had made since they met, but if she had anything to say about it, she lost the chance.

"There it is!" she exclaimed, spying their destination. At least they had beat the rain and would soon be out of the threatening winds.

Garth cut the speed and tested the approach carefully so as not to run aground. The tidewaters were often deceptive, hiding sand banks just below the surface. Meanwhile, Deirdre concentrated her full effort on sighting the cabin, or at least another boat that might have been dragged ashore and hidden among the trees. She saw nothing.

"They're not here," she told him, feeling defeated.

"Someone might have dropped them off," Garth suggested. "His fishing friends, perhaps."

"I don't think so. Danny's little brother would have told me, knowing how concerned I was."

"Don't bet on it, honey. Kids have a way of sticking together even when they're squealing on each other."

They tied up at the small dock, which was in desperate need of repair. Garth climbed out first, then extended his hand to Deirdre, which she gladly took. The wind was unbelievably strong now, or perhaps it just seemed worse on the open and unprotected peninsula.

"The cabin must be over there, hidden behind those trees," Deirdre called loudly, trying to be heard above the wind. "It's been so long, I honestly can't remember."

Garth slid a supporting arm around her waist, drawing her protectively to his side. "Come on," he urged. "We'll find it."

To Deirdre's relief, the cabin was precisely where she had guessed. The wooden porch creaked under their weight, but the door swung open on a well-oiled hinge. The one room was empty, but it looked lived in and perfectly ordered.

Deirdre stood just inside the door, engulfed in the semidarkness. Slowly her eyes adjusted and she made out the shapes of the sparse furnishings. A wood-burning stove sat near the corner and beside that was an old, worn wood rocker. There was a small sofa that had clearly seen better days, and a low table that held an assortment of magazines and hardcover books.

Deirdre turned to find Garth lighting an oil-burning lantern. With the aid of the light she could see the other furnishings that occupied the room, but she lost interest in such exploration when her eyes fell on a table pushed up against the far wall. On the top sat a row of framed photographs that made her heart wrench with pain. The smiling, loving faces of Craig's parents stared back at her, and beside this was a group portrait of their small family.

Deirdre walked steadily toward the table, leaving Garth to look around on his own. She had almost forgotten what they looked like, Deirdre thought as she touched the faces in the pictures. How vague those memories were now: her aunt and uncle . . . her own mother . . . even her father. She hadn't allowed herself to dwell on the past, but she was certain of one thing. Craig had not forgotten. If she needed proof of that fact, it was in these pictures. Not one was of Craig after his parents died.

Deirdre had thought searching Craig's room had been an invasion of privacy, but that didn't begin to compare to being here. She felt as though they had stepped into Craig's private thoughts, the thoughts he could share with no one.

It wasn't until Garth came to stand beside her that Deirdre realized her face was wet with tears. Tears were futile, she knew, but she couldn't have stopped them if she tried. She couldn't remember a time when she'd ever been so overwhelmed by emotion. Not when Steven rejected her; not even the loss of her parents had affected her as profoundly as the discovery that Craig had been coming here all these years, and she never once suspected.

Garth lifted the group picture from the table and studied it closely. Swallowing back the tears, Deirdre said,

"That's Craig and his parents. They died in a fire when Craig was small." Deirdre sniffed indelicately and a sob escaped from her throat. "His father got Craig out, then went back for Craig's mother. Craig . . . saw it all." Deirdre closed her eyes tightly. "My God, what that must have done to him. I never realized," she sobbed convulsively. "If I'd known, I could have . . ."

She couldn't go on but she didn't need to. Garth knew instinctively how she was feeling, and after replacing the picture on the table, he reached out and drew her into his arms.

"Don't do this to yourself, Deirdre," he said softly, hugging her close as he spoke. "There are people who simply can't share parts of their lives with others. This place is like that for Craig. It's a wonderful place, filled with wonderful memories of his parents."

"I know," she murmured. "But I thought I knew him so well."

Clinging to his strength, Deirdre cried until her emotion was spent. It had been a long time since she had allowed herself the luxury of tears, and even longer since she had allowed herself to feel as close to a man as she felt to Garth in those long moments spent in his arms. She reveled in the comfort. Not because she was indulging in a moment of self-pity, but because she was able to gain a better understanding of the man she had been so overwhelmingly attracted to from the first moment she saw him. He was strong yet sensitive, confident, and yet in his own way he was as vulnerable as she was at that moment. He made no attempt to release her or to move away from her even though the moment for comfort had passed.

Indeed, his hands stroked the length of her back and seemed to mold her closer to him. With her face buried against his chest, Deirdre easily felt the steady increase of his heartbeat. She felt a curious sense of power, knowing she was responsible for this change in him. She had elicited the same emotions from him as he had from her, and it was happening without either of them intending for it to.

"Deirdre," Garth whispered, his dark cheek brushing the top of her hair as his hands moved to her shoulders. Deirdre's hands unclasped from around his waist and when he was finally able to put some distance between them, she allowed her hands to rest momentarily at his waist.

Deirdre looked up at him, her eyes still feverishly bright from the tears. She knew then that she wanted a great deal more from Garth than just comfort, and she could see in his eyes that his thoughts were rapidly taking the same course.

But that didn't stop him from releasing her completely, then turning and walking away. "It looks like we're in for a stormy night." Just as ambiguously, he added, "I'll see what I can do about getting a fire started."

I think you already have, Deirdre thought, but wisely she kept silent. She didn't know why, but she realized Garth Logan would fight this growing desire between them.

Chapter Three

Deirdre looked down at her empty teacup, and wondered why she had the sudden urge to cry. She hadn't let herself think about that night in a very long time. Now she didn't seem to have much choice in the matter, as the memory was flooding back of its own volition. She was forced to recount the long hours she had spent falling helplessly in love with Garth, and she blamed it on the knowledge that Garth had returned. How ironic, she thought, that just when she feared she might have to tell her inquisitive son the truth—that he might never see his father—Garth should come back.

Testing herself, Deirdre tried mustering up some of her old feelings for Garth. But those feelings had lain dormant too long. She would be seeing Garth again very soon, but as hard as she tried, she couldn't seem to care. Watching Andy grow had numbed her to the pain of having their child alone. She had needed Garth desperately to help her through the fear of having their child, the fear of losing him when he was born prematurely, and above all, the fear of what the future held for them: the ultimate contrast to her well-ordered past.

But long before Andy was born, Deirdre realized that her life would never be the same again. How could it be, once she had begun to fall in love with Garth Logan?

That night, they had sat by the fire and talked for what seemed like hours. Garth made her understand why Craig hadn't told her about coming to the cabin. Oddly enough, he also helped her to understand why Craig wouldn't have confided in her about his relationship with Jasamin Grant. Craig was much more of a private person than she had ever thought and she vowed to respect that in the future. Jasamin Grant, she decided, must be extremely important to Craig. Suddenly Deirdre found herself becoming more curious about the girl, and what her relationship was to Garth. Garth identified her as his ward, and he obviously wasn't wild about having the responsibility. Nevertheless, he had accepted it and clearly took such responsibility seriously. Deirdre couldn't help but wonder if there wasn't something more to it. Something Garth wasn't telling her.

With her legs curled up beneath her on the sofa, Deirdre studied Garth closely as he sat in the rocking chair, examining the books Craig had left on the table.

"If that picture you showed me does her justice, I would say Jasamin Grant is a very beautiful girl," Deirdre remarked, hoping to sound casual rather than overtly interested.

Garth didn't look up from his selection of reading material. "Jasamin? Oh, yes, I guess she's pretty enough," he remarked absently. "Your cousin has rather diversified taste in books. Charles Dickens and Jack London," he said with a mild laugh. "Very interesting. Did you know you can judge a person's character fairly accurately by the type of books he reads?"

Deirdre didn't know if she was more annoyed because he so easily avoided discussing Jasamin Grant or because his remark seemed critical of Craig's character. She was far too sensitive on both subjects.

"For your information, those books were part of *my* collection."

His eyes lifted and he smiled warmly at her. "I never would have guessed," he said, lowering his eyes over her appreciatively. "I would have thought you were more the love-story type. You know, lots of passion and tears but always a happy ending."

Deirdre's chin lifted. "Well, you're wrong!" she lied,

bristling with the knowledge he could read her so well. "I happen to be a realist, Mr. Logan."

Garth laughed. "Does that mean you don't believe in love?"

Lowering her feet to the floor, Deirdre shifted into a more comfortable position. Odd how she'd been perfectly comfortable until that moment. Why would such a simple question unnerve her so?

"Aren't you going to answer me, Deirdre?" he prodded gently.

Her eyes met his. "Yes, I believe in love. I was engaged once, but it didn't work out."

Garth was silent for a moment, then asked quite seriously, "Who broke it off?"

Deirdre didn't shy away from the subject as she had in the past. Without realizing precisely when it had happened, Steven had been relegated to a very *distant* past.

"He did, as a matter of fact," she admitted.

Garth smiled again and muttered what she thought was, "The man's a fool," before taking his book up again.

For the next half hour Deirdre busied herself by searching through the tinned foods in the cabinets for the makings of a meal. The storm showed no sign of abating, and Deirdre knew it would be too dark to return soon in any case. But suddenly, the prospect of spending the night in the cabin was no longer quite so unappealing.

"Are you hungry?" she asked Garth as she examined the battered cooking utensils in the kitchen.

Garth crossed the room to stand beside the counter where she worked. "Now that you mention it, I'm starved. Any coffee in the cabinet?"

"Just instant, but at least there's bottled water to make it with."

"Good enough," said Garth, beginning a systematic search of the utility cabinet. His search uncovered several items they would be needing later, such as sheets and blankets. Both were in adequate supply, Deirdre noticed. But now that he had that problem solved, she mused silently, where was he going to find the separate beds to put them on?

Suddenly, Deirdre realized just how wrong she had been in her initial judgment of Garth. His work was in Central America—why had she envisioned a social whirl of nightclubs and society women? Aside from that, he had flown all the way here to find his runaway ward. Hardly the act of a carefree playboy. And, finally, any interest he had in Deirdre personally was kept carefully in check. She doubted the words "casual affair" were part of his vocabulary.

Just as well, thought Deirdre as they dined in companionable silence. She certainly wasn't the sort to sleep with a man simply because she was physically attracted to him. Still, she knew if Garth Logan were to present her with that opportunity, she wouldn't be able to say no quite as easily as she had with the other men in her past.

A warm glow from the fireplace and the dim lantern enveloped them as they ate their meal. By the time Deirdre reached for her coffee she was perfectly content. Curled up on the sofa opposite from Garth, she was only vaguely aware that the storm had begun to recede in the past half-hour and was leaving a calm breeze in its wake.

"You haven't said much about your job," prompted Deirdre. "Is it dangerous?" she asked, having read more than enough magazine articles about the violent undercurrent that set the tone of life throughout much of Central America.

Garth shrugged, but by no means did his expression indicate indifference to the subject. "I try not to think about it, but, yes, it can be dangerous. Foreign governments don't always take kindly to outside intervention, particularly within the labor force. For the most part, ensuring your safety lies in choosing your friends carefully, and . . . in not wearing your hair too long. It could get you mistaken for a guerrilla soldier and shot on sight." Deirdre folded her hands in her lap but not before Garth noticed them trembling. Suddenly he smiled. "Incidents like that aren't all that common, Deirdre. I didn't mean to frighten you."

Deirdre managed to still her hands. "I just hadn't realized," she explained, unwilling to admit how important he was becoming to her. She was beginning to feel close to him . . . afraid for him . . . and that would never do! "Why do you do it, Garth? Is your work that important to you?"

His attention was held by the flicker of the lamplight as he spoke. "Yes, it's important to me. It's more than just negotiating contracts. Before I agreed to this assignment, I was just another lawyer, burning myself out on work that I had no interest in. I'm good at what I do," he said without vanity. "I can't imagine wanting to do anything else or . . ." He paused, then said quietly, "Or be anywhere else."

Deirdre looked at him searchingly and drew his gaze to her. She couldn't help but ask boldly, "Is that why you're divorced?"

Garth wasn't angered by the probing question. Perhaps he realized she hadn't meant to sound accusing or critical.

He walked over to the window and stared out at the descending darkness. "Yes, Deirdre, that's precisely why I'm divorced," he said thickly. Whether he was angry or not, he clearly wasn't pleased that she had asked.

His statement raised even more questions about him in Deirdre's mind. Was she to assume that, because he had chosen his work over his marriage, he would choose his work over any relationship? Was that why he had revealed his personal feelings about his job? If he had done so to discourage her, he couldn't have chosen a more effective way of accomplishing his goal. Strange, Deirdre thought, how one minute she could see him as totally honest and unselfish, and the next, she could resent him for his arrogance in assuming she was interested in him in the first place!

"The storm is letting up," said Deirdre abruptly, pushing herself from the sofa. "I'm going out to check the boat and make sure it hasn't sunk under all this rain."

Garth turned from the window. "I'll check it, Deirdre. You stay inside."

She turned a haughty gaze at him. "I'm perfectly capable, Mr. Logan!" she snapped without meaning to. "I can manage quite nicely without a man around."

With that, Deirdre flung open the door and walked out, anxious to put some distance between them. If ever she needed time to be alone with her thoughts, this was it.

The threatening wind had now subsided and a gentle breeze caressed Deirdre's face. It took her only a few minutes to realize she was more angry with herself than she was with Garth. The transition from girl to woman hadn't been any major feat for Deirdre, but that was only because she had failed at one very important part of the transition. She hadn't learned how to play the cat-and-mouse game other women her age were so accomplished at. In that respect, Deirdre bore the innocence of a young girl. Garth was a man she was very much attracted to, and she was at a loss as to what to do about it.

After pumping the boat free of water, Deirdre didn't return immediately to the cabin. She sank down on the wet, grassy slope of the shoreline and watched as the last glimmer of light faded from the sky. The air smelled fresh after the rain and the rich scent of earth permeated her nostrils. In the far distance, Deirdre could see the storm moving west, the flashes of lightning illuminating the dark, billowy clouds.

With her knees drawn up to her chest, Deirdre buried her face and told herself, not for the first time since leaving the cabin so abruptly, that she shouldn't have pried so deeply into his personal life. Garth's divorce was none of her business. He was nothing to her, she repeated to her weary heart with finality. But her heart wasn't buying it any more than her mind had. Like a complete fool, she was falling for him and she was helpless to do anything about it.

"Didn't your mother ever tell you not to sit on the ground during a month that has an *r* in it?" Garth had come up behind her so quietly, his voice startled her for a moment. "You'll catch cold for sure," he added, sitting down beside her.

Deirdre managed a smile. "My mother was never one to put much stock in old wives' tales. Apparently, yours wasn't either," she added, fully conscious of his nearness. Within touching distance, she thought, clasping her fingers tightly together around her knees.

"I was never what one would call an obedient child," he mused as he stroked her cheek with a wildflower he'd picked on the way. He motioned for her to take it, and she did, examining the moisture on the bright yellow petals.

"Peace offering," said Garth.

Deirdre glanced up quickly, but her expression was guarded. "Are we at war?"

"I'm not sure. By rights we should be at odds over this situation between Jasamin and Craig, but I find I like pulling with you better than pushing against you."

Deirdre sighed with disgust. "I should have known that even seeing Craig's cabin wouldn't change your opinion of him."

Garth leaned back on his elbows. "Craig is eighteen, Deirdre, and in my book that's old enough to take responsibility for his actions. Jasamin is a young girl, just trying her wings. According to the law, she's still a child."

"Do you do everything by the book?" Deirdre's frown showed her disappointment at his unyielding stand against Craig.

Garth shrugged. "That's pretty much my job."

"No quarter for human failing, is that it? You discount emotion simply because you never lose control yourself."

"Is that what you think?" His words were as challenging as his eyes, and Deirdre looked away. What would he do, she wondered, if she tried seducing him to prove her point?

"Yes," she returned coolly. "That's precisely what I think. You haven't even considered the possibility that those two kids might really love each other, or at least think they do," she conceded to his doubting glance. "The point is, Craig is also trying his wings and it's just possible your ward conned him into this little adventure."

"That's entirely possible, knowing Jasamin. But that's not the law, is it?"

"Oh, blast the law!" Deirdre cried angrily. "Haven't you ever done anything in your life that you regretted?"

Garth thought a moment and Deirdre could easily see he wasn't taking this discussion half as seriously as she was.

"No," he said blandly. "I can't think of one thing."

Deirdre's eyes narrowed. "What about your marriage?" she dared to suggest, even though that subject had already caused her one unpleasant moment. "Need I remind you it ended in divorce?"

"Too true," Garth mused, apparently not in the least offended. "But I don't regret that. Both the marriage and the divorce were quite agreeable and not the least unpleasant."

Deirdre stared incredulously. "I can see why you're a lawyer."

Garth laughed huskily, then sat up again and leaned slightly toward her. "These are the facts, Deirdre. Men are generally aware of the pleasures of sex before women are. Therefore, it stands to reason that men should be the ones to take the responsibility for it. A girl Jasamin's age is experimenting with sex. A *man* Craig's age knows exactly what he's doing."

As she digested this line of reasoning, Deirdre moistened her upper lip with her tongue, unaware of how provocative the gesture was. She was, however, acutely aware of the provocative action that followed. Lifting the flower Garth had given her, Deirdre stroked the sensuous curve of his lips with the petals.

"Tell me something, Garth," she said, using her most

alluring tone of voice. "How old does a woman have to be before she shares the responsibility?"

Garth was momentarily surprised by her gesture, but he was far too experienced, she decided, not to realize when he was being deliberately provoked, rather than seduced. He smiled and stared deeply into her eyes.

"You're old enough, Deirdre Mallory. That's something I have become increasingly aware of."

Deirdre continued to stare at him, pleased he would make such an admission. She lowered her eyes to the sensuous curve of his mouth, wondering how he would react if she leaned toward him and pressed her lips to his. She didn't get the chance to find out.

"But this has nothing to do with Jasamin and Craig," Garth stated abruptly. He moved his eyes away uncomfortably. "Jasamin is the sort of girl who dives into twenty feet of water and then remembers she can't swim. Invariably she cries out for help, and so far there's always been someone around to save her."

"Are you saying she gets herself into this sort of trouble all the time?" Deirdre asked.

"No, of course not!" He sounded defensive, which made Deirdre much more curious about his protectiveness for the girl. "I only meant that she thrives on attention. She's really very insecure."

Deirdre had her doubts about that, knowing Jasamin Grant was very rich as well as very beautiful, but she kept her doubts to herself. Instead, she asked, "Does she thrive on anyone's attention, Garth? Or just on yours?"

She knew her words had found their mark when Garth moved away abruptly. He stood and walked to the edge of the shoreline and said, "You have enough to worry about with Craig. I suggest you leave Jasamin to me."

Deirdre stood, shocked by the acid in his tone. Had she really said something to warrant his contempt, or had she merely underestimated how far Garth Logan would go to protect his so-called fragile ward?

Walking over to him, she tucked the stem of the wildflower into the welt pocket of his shirt. Her message was clear. The battle lines were drawn and the sides were chosen.

"There are no running lights on the boat," she said coolly, "so we can't go back tonight. I trust that won't be too uncomfortable for you."

"Deirdre," said Garth gruffly, catching her arm when she started to walk away. He sighed heavily and shook his head. "I'm sorry. Look, I know this isn't your fault. You've done your best to help, and I really don't mean to take my frustrations out on you."

"I'm sure you don't." Deirdre spoke truthfully, but she doubted he believed that as she pulled hastily from his grip. She'd do anything to conceal how responsive she was to him even when the tension crackled between them.

Garth made no attempt to follow her from the clearing, but Deirdre wasn't unhappy returning to the cabin alone. With any luck she would be asleep before the mosquitoes drove Garth in for the night. As far as Deirdre was concerned, the sooner they returned home and parted company, the better.

There was a freshwater storage tank outside the house and, although Deirdre suspected the water wasn't pure enough to drink from, she knew it would at least suffice for washing the dishes and providing her with an adequate bath before bed. Surely Garth would give her that much time alone.

Taking a bucket down from the peg, she held it under the spout and prized open the nozzle. The bucket filled slowly and her arms ached from holding it, but eventually the bucket was filled and she reached up with one hand to close the nozzle once again. She hadn't counted on it jamming. By the time she thought to set the bucket down so that she could work with both hands, the entire front of her shirt was soaked through.

"Oh, no," Deirdre groaned at the same time a roar of laughter reached her from the edge of the clearing.

"May I be of assistance?" Garth asked, stepping aside

so that he got little more than a splash of water on his shoes. He closed the valve with one hand, adding to Deirdre's smoldering anger.

"That bucket looks a little small for a bath," Garth teased, clearly forgetting the argument they'd had only a few minutes before.

Deirdre hadn't forgotten, and that, combined with the frustration of being isolated with a man that had her emotions in a turmoil, caused her to react vindictively. Before she even thought to stop herself, she had thrown the water at him, leaving him thoroughly soaked.

"You're right, Garth," she said smartly. "It is a little small for a bath."

"Why you vicious little . . ." The epithet died on his lips as Deirdre turned away smugly. "Oh, no, you don't," he said menacingly, catching her arm seconds before she could slip away.

Deirdre imagined a hundred things he could do to get her back, but not for a moment did she imagine being pulled to his chest with such force. She cried out breathlessly as he pinned her arms between his own. With one arm wrapped around her back, Garth tangled his free hand in the mass of her burnished-copper hair, preventing her from turning her face away. His mouth came down hard on her sensitive, startled lips and even if Deirdre had wanted to break the kiss, her strength was no match for his.

But what began as a vengeful, punishing assault soon became a masterfully executed invasion of the senses. With a will of its own, Deirdre's body curved to the masculine contours of his, responding in the only possible manner to the compelling touch of his hands.

I never knew this was possible, thought Deirdre, parting her lips eagerly to the probing delectation of his tongue. To be so thoroughly drawn into the embrace of a man—the thought of it ending was incomprehensible. How could I have ever thought his kisses would be average, his lovemaking disappointing?

Her arms were freed suddenly and she wrapped them around his neck and clung to him feverishly. All she could think of now was that if she'd married Steven Blake, she would have never known this kind of wanting.

Later, in retrospect, Deirdre would plead temporary insanity to justify that moment in his arms. There was no other explanation for the way she returned his hungry kisses and pressed herself to the hardness of his body until the cold dampness of their clothing was overwhelmed by the heat of their embrace.

A low moan escaped her lips as Garth worked the top few buttons on her shirt, lowering his mouth to caress the exposed flesh gently. Deirdre arched her neck, moving her shoulders slightly back as the nerve endings along her spine commanded. By the time his tongue found the sensitive hollow between her breasts, Deirdre could scarcely breathe.

Garth's hand moved beneath her shirt, but paused just below the swell of her breast. Seconds later, his head lifted at the same time Deirdre felt the muscles of his back begin to tighten and pull away.

"I'm sorry, Deirdre," he said as his taut fingers left her warm, aroused flesh. He moved slowly, as if he wanted to continue touching her but was denying himself the pleasure.

"I didn't mean for that to happen," he said, taking a deep breath. "You make a man forget his good intentions very easily."

She knew he wasn't apologizing for kissing her. He was only sorry he had let it get out of control. But Deirdre wasn't sorry. She was only confused.

"I don't understand, Garth. In the cabin, when you were holding me, I felt . . . I mean, I sensed that you wanted to . . ."

His head lifted and his eyes darted back to her, cutting her off in mid-sentence. "You sensed what, Deirdre? That I've been thinking about how much I'd like to sleep with you since the first moment I laid eyes on you?" Deirdre made no attempt to deny this, even though the most she had sensed in him was a guarded interest.

"Well, you'd be right, Deirdre. And if I'd met you under any other circumstances, I probably wouldn't hesitate."

Deirdre felt a tightening in her chest. "Are you saying that because of Jasamin and Craig—"

"God, no!" Garth exclaimed, shaking his head. "I'm saying it's because I've gotten to know you these past few hours. You're not the type of woman a man walks away from after he's made love to her. Whether you know it or not, that makes you a very dangerous lady to know. You're not a one-night stand, Deirdre," he said, his gaze smoldering now as it penetrated hers. "And when tomorrow comes . . . I *have* to walk away."

Deirdre knew he was right, but it didn't make her feel any better. He had just paid her one of the finest compliments a man could give a woman, but instead of being touched that he would hold her in such high regard, all she could think about was the pain of rejection. That and the humiliation she felt for having responded to his lovemaking with such desperation.

"I hope you don't expect me to thank you for that," she said, meeting his gaze evenly. His eyes widened and a deep crease parted his brows, but she went on undaunted. "You're very self-righteous when it's to your benefit, Garth. It's not my feelings you're concerned about, it's your own! Or, to be more precise, you're afraid you'll have to compromise that unyielding desire you have to punish Craig if you go to bed with his cousin."

"That's ridiculous and you know it!" Garth snapped angrily.

"Is it?" Deirdre's brow arched sharply. "One minute you were kissing me like a man who had a very definite purpose in mind, and then you stopped. Did you suddenly remember you were holding one of the enemy in your arms?"

"Why, you provocative little witch!" He was seething,

his control threatening to snap completely. "You're the most maddening creature I've ever met. I pity the man who does finally get you."

Deirdre's eyes widened as if she'd been struck. "What's that supposed to mean?"

Deirdre hadn't noticed the way the damp front of her shirt clung to her body, but now Garth's lowered eyes made her all too aware of it. The cotton shirt had gently molded itself to the swell of her breasts, and although she wore a bra, it too was whisper thin. Damp as it was, it only aided in the exposure of the woman underneath in vivid detail.

"You have a delectable body, Deirdre," Garth said, smiling as she attempted, rather unsuccessfully, to pull the revealing fabric away from her skin. "You're too damn beautiful to be believed, although I doubt you're even aware of it. And you have the most expressive green eyes I've ever seen. They've been sending out the same message from the moment we met. One way or another, Deirdre Mallory, you're going to cause some man a lot of sleepless nights."

Deirdre didn't need a mirror to know what he was talking about. Steven had always told her she had expressive eyes, but he had generally noticed them only when she was angry with him about something. What Garth read in her eyes was something entirely different. But what Garth didn't know was that he alone had put it there. As close as she had been to Steven, he had never been able to make her feel the way Garth had in the few hours she'd known him. And when Garth left, Deirdre was confident no man would ever see that look in her eyes again.

Why did it have to be him? Deirdre wondered. Why did I have to fall in love with a man like Garth Logan?

"Would you help me draw some more water?" she asked, bringing their futile conversation to an abrupt halt. "I'd like to wash before going to bed."

It was a moment before he answered. "The bath's already set up. I did it while you were out checking the boat. You'll find water heating on the stove."

Deirdre walked into the cabin and found everything just as he had said she would, and then some. The sofa was folded out into a bed that would sleep two comfortably, but Deirdre was certain it would sleep only one that night. Garth had also hooked up a rope and sheet to provide privacy for her bath. Strangely enough, Deirdre was able to smile at this. Garth might find her a "maddening creature," but that was nothing to the way she thought of him. He was truly one of a kind.

Deirdre had just begun to remove her clothes behind the sheet when she heard the door open and Garth come inside. Neither spoke, but Deirdre found it awkward with him being there. When she heard him settling into the creaking rocking chair on the other side of the room, she turned her full attention back to her bath.

Garth picked up a book and began to flip through it, attempting to ignore the silhouette cast against the sheet by the firelight. Within minutes, his gaze lifted again and he froze. Deirdre had unbuttoned her shirt and peeled it off her back. The oversized shirt had disguised her womanly figure, but as each article of clothing was removed, what lay beneath became harder to ignore.

Deirdre reveled in the warmth from the stove as she drew the soapy washcloth over her shoulders and arms. The tips of her breasts responded to the coarse material of the cloth just as they had responded to the feel of Garth's body earlier. Her flesh began to tingle with the awareness that he was sitting only a few feet away. She tossed her hair back with a shake of her head in an effort to push all thoughts of Garth from her mind, but the effort was futile.

Deirdre was startled when she heard the thud of a book hitting the table. "Dickens or Jack London?" she asked, smiling to herself.

"Neither," he grumbled strangely. "Could you hurry up, Deirdre? I'd like to get some sleep tonight."

"I'll only be a few minutes," she told him. "I consider bathing one of life's greatest pleasures." She couldn't resist taunting.

Garth muttered something she didn't catch and then blurted out, "If you're going to take all night, we might as well talk. What sort of man was this guy you were going to marry?" In light of their previous conversation, Deirdre thought this a strange question, but, assuming he was just making idle conversation, she saw no reason not to answer.

"Steven was very nice," she said. "My father liked him."

Garth laughed. "What about you? Did you like him or didn't that matter?"

Deirdre made a sour face. "Well, of course I liked him! In fact, I loved him very much, or at least I thought I did." It's not the same, Deirdre acknowledged silently. "It wasn't long after he broke our engagement that I realized I was more disillusioned than hurt."

"Why was that?" Garth's tone was more inquisitive now.

Deirdre reached for a towel. "Steven was the only man I had ever known," she explained, not needing to clarify the intimacy of their relationship. "We had what people considered a perfect romance. Steven came from a wealthy background and, although we weren't rich, my father's family were one of the town's original founders. Steven wanted to be a doctor, which he now is," she said wryly, "and I planned on following in my father's footsteps. He was a college professor. History. We had it all worked out—I would be home much of the time with the children, but I could have a career as well." Deirdre laughed gaily. "See what I mean by an ideal relationship? Our lives were so perfectly mapped out, it was more like a fairy tale than reality."

"What went wrong?" Garth asked curiously.

Deirdre clutched the towel to her breast, regretting the direction this conversation had taken.

"My father died that summer," she said sadly. "Steven . . . well, he just decided he didn't want the responsibility of a ready-made family."

"Craig, you mean," Garth persisted, his tone giving no indication of his feelings on the subject.

"Yes, that's right. He didn't want Craig living with us after we were married."

Garth remained thoughtfully silent for some moments. "What about your education, Deirdre? I take it you didn't earn your degree?"

"No, I didn't even start college. But it didn't really matter, since I was working at a summer job I liked very much. My boss is very nice and when my father died, she offered me a permanent position. It's a dress shop in town," she explained. "I really love working there, and someday I'd like to own it."

Deirdre wrapped the towel around her torso and tucked the fold between her breasts, then stepped out from behind the sheet. She left it hanging, assuming Garth wanted to use it as well, but he gave no such indication as his eyes surveyed her incredulously. His scrutiny had nothing to do with the fact that she wore only a brief towel. It was her confession that incited him.

"You gave up a college education to work in a dress shop?" He clearly found this inconceivable. How could he be so sensitive and understanding one minute, and sound like such a snob the next?

"It's not *just* a dress shop. It's a boutique!"

"I stand corrected," he sneered.

"I don't think you realize how important Craig is to me. He's like my own brother, and he would have done the same thing for me. Any sacrifices I've made have been worth it, and that includes Mr. Steven Blake," she said haughtily. "I would do it all over again without question."

Garth rolled his eyes in disbelief. "This Joan of Arc nobility is admirable, Deirdre, but that doesn't justify denying Craig a male influence in his life when it was most crucial."

Deirdre couldn't resist laughing. "By male influence I assume you mean someone a young boy can kick a football around with? Mr. Logan, no one would ever accuse you of being a feminist."

Garth rose from the chair, not the least bit amused. "Don't be an idiot, Deirdre. You know that has nothing to do with it. Craig might well be, at this very moment, married to a seventeen-year-old girl. It's obvious he has absolutely no sense of responsibility."

Deirdre's brow arched sharply. "As far as I'm concerned, he's being very responsible if he's at least willing to marry the girl."

Garth shook his head and sighed resolutely. If he expected her to condone such an unyielding and unreasonable attitude toward Craig—and blame him for this whole mess simply because he was legally of age—he was very much mistaken. Besides, Deirdre knew intuitively that there was more to this girl Jasamin than Garth was admitting.

"You are by far the most stubborn female I've met in my life," Garth remarked, squaring his shoulders before turning away.

Deirdre smiled and laughed softly, watching as he walked over to take the sheet off the line. "Well," she chimed lightly, "I suppose that's better than 'maddening creature.' You haven't exactly done wonders for my ego up till now."

Garth turned to face her, but his expression was unreadable. His eyes moved slowly over her as he obviously undressed her mentally. The towel didn't leave much to his imagination. With a little nerve, thought Deirdre, she could release the tuck and the towel would fall away. But she lacked the courage, and she suspected Garth knew this. But she doubted that he realized that she was frozen not because of her damaged ego, but because her heart couldn't bear the pain of another rejection.

"Should we flip a coin to see which of us takes the bed?" Deirdre asked, collecting the fragments of her dignity as well as she could. If Garth had begun to think of her as a casual fling, she had no one to blame but herself. But if that were true, why wasn't she feeling guilty for presenting the temptation in the first place?

"You take the bed," said Garth, rubbing his hand wearily over the nape of his neck. "I'll be fine in the chair."

Deirdre walked over to the far side of the bed as Garth turned to extinguish the lantern. The firelight immediately enveloped them in its soft glow, and suddenly, as if drawn by a magnet, their eyes met across the width of the bed. Deirdre knew at that moment that the slightest weakening of reserve, on either of their parts, would prove their undoing. Their reason for being stranded together was suddenly insignificant, as Deidre could easily see Garth wanted her as much as she wanted him.

She didn't ask him why he wasn't removing his own wet clothes. She doubted he would believe that she was asking merely out of concern. Instead she slipped into the bed and drew the blanket over her.

Deirdre turned on her side, with her back to him. She used the crook of her arm for a pillow, but was unable to relax enough to go to sleep. She heard him moving around and then settling into the chair. She listened for a sound that might lull her to sleep, but the only thing she heard was the crackle of the fire and that didn't help at all. It only reminded her of the way Garth looked by firelight, with the gold light dancing off his tobacco-brown hair and adding a feverish brightness to his rich brandy-colored eyes. His bronzed flesh radiated a glow that reminded her of the warmth and comfort she had felt when he first held her in his arms.

Deirdre closed her eyes to block out the image, but it was only magnified. Oh, God, she thought, this is madness. It would come to nothing. Garth would find his ward tomorrow and he would be gone from her life for good. It was unfair to have met a man like Garth, a man who could disrupt her life so easily.

"You're going to freeze over there, Deirdre," Garth said softly. "You should sleep closer to the fire."

"I'm all right," she said, and then wished she had pretended to be asleep and not answered at all.

"Are you? Then why are you trembling?"

Holding herself still, Deirdre pulled the blanket up over her shoulder. "I guess I am cold," she said. Then, throwing caution to the wind, she turned to face him. "Make me warm, Garth."

The request was spoken so softly, she half hoped, half feared that he hadn't heard. But he had, and he remained motionless in the chair.

"I want you, Deirdre, but it wouldn't—"

"I know," she cut in, resting her head against her arm. "You're scared it would mean more for me than it would for you. But I'm not asking for more than you can give, Garth."

"But you deserve more. You have a right to expect more." He was breathing huskily.

There was a silence and then Deirdre gently folded back the blanket, saying, "Let me be the judge of that."

After a moment Garth left the chair. With the golden glow of the fire behind him, Deirdre watched as he removed his shirt, exposing the wide expanse of his deeply bronzed chest. He hesitated over the belt of his slacks, but the hesitation was brief and seconds later he stood before her unclothed.

Deirdre felt no shyness at his nakedness. Indeed, she stared openly, committing every detail of his well-formed body to memory. Strong cords of muscle rippled down his arms and squared thickly across his chest. Garth was a man well familiar with hard, physical labor, in spite of the fact that he had what was technically a desk job. A thick, curling mat of light brown hair covered his chest, tapering spearlike down his middle. There was a taut flatness to his stomach and a leanness to his hips and thighs that revealed solid muscle as he moved like a sleek jungle animal toward the bed.

When Garth joined her on the bed, Deirdre reached out immediately and touched his throat and then his shoulders, as if to assure herself he was real and not just some image her dreams had created.

"Deirdre . . . are you sure?" Garth said huskily, extending a hand to touch her in the same manner. "If you're not sure—"

Deirdre placed her fingertips against his lips. "I've never been so sure of anything in my life."

Garth bent his head and took her lips briefly as he eased the blanket away from her. The towel was still between them when he pulled her to him, but it didn't keep her from feeling the warmth and desire emanating from his body.

Deirdre slipped a hand behind his head, smiling as the thickness of his hair tingled against her palm. "It's crazy, the little things a woman will notice about a man she's attracted to."

Garth smiled down at her, lifting his hand to release the tuck of her towel. "Like what?" he asked, extending a finger to trail between her breasts as the towel eased away.

Deirdre's hand slid from his hair to his chest, where she began a gentle massage. "The thickness and the texture of your hair, for instance," she said softly, tracing a circular pattern in the hair that grew there. "Also," she whispered, pressing her face against his throat, "I've memorized your scent. You smell clean and healthy like a man should."

Garth laughed softly. "And you smell very much like a practical soap," he teased as he stripped the towel away completely so his hands could move freely over her nakedness. "But you feel very much like a woman," he breathed, moving against her again with a surge of passion.

His mouth took hers again and her lips parted eagerly,

inviting the exploration of his tongue. An electric current shot through Deirdre at that moment, banishing her fear that he felt nothing special for her. His kisses were too thorough, too passionate to mean nothing.

His mouth left hers suddenly and he eased away from her to survey the body his hands were exploring so intimately. "You're more beautiful than I'd imagined," he said, bringing his hand to cup her swelling breast. His mouth lowered to taste the nipple his hand had aroused to peak hardness, eliciting a moan of pleasure from deep within her.

When his hand swept over the alluring curve of her hip, Deirdre responded even more urgently and allowed her own hands to explore the taut muscles of his shoulders and back, and gently stroke the flesh that covered his waist and hips.

"Oh, God," Garth groaned, drawing her against him and burying his face against her throat. He rolled onto his back and her supple body matched the contour of his own.

Arched against him, Deirdre lifted her head so that her long hair fell over one shoulder. Her breasts were glistening with the moistness he had applied, and Garth held her there, stretching his long fingers to cover as much flesh as possible while he guided her against him.

Sliding his hands over the curve of her hips, Garth applied gentle pressure and drew her down to him, so he could drink from her intoxicating lips once again.

"Love me," Deirdre moaned against his searching lips. "Oh, Garth, love me," she pleaded, the cry dragged from the depths of her being, her conscious mind unable to suppress it.

Garth rolled over with her again, parting her thighs with his own. Deirdre gave only the most fleeting thought to Steven and the way it had been between them. There was no basis for comparison and she wouldn't even try. Her love for Garth was all-consuming, and she gave herself to it eagerly.

The impassioned cry, when it came, mingled with his own against her mouth, and from that moment Deirdre knew she would never belong solely to herself again. Just as surely as she had crossed the bounds of womanhood, Garth had laid claim to her body and soul.

Deirdre lay in his arms, marveling at the small sounds she now heard in the quiet night: the crackling of the fire, the croak of a lone bullfrog outside, the singing of crickets, and the sound of Garth's heart drumming beneath her ear.

They hadn't spoken since he had moved away from her. Words didn't seem necessary, and Deirdre didn't want anything said that would break the spell enveloping them.

Garth spread his hand over her back, hugging her close to him as though he, too, were remembering the way it had been between them. "I watched your silhouette behind the sheet while you were bathing," he said softly. "I couldn't take my eyes off you, even though I knew this might happen."

Deirdre smiled and pressed her lips to his chest. "I know," she admitted quietly. When she lifted her head, she saw the delight in his eyes.

"What am I going to do with you, sweet witch," he teased, and in response, Deirdre moved her bent leg over the lower half of his body.

"Deirdre," Garth murmured, his eyes closing from the sheer ecstasy her aggressive act brought him. He spoke her name again against her mouth, the utterance becoming a caress as a renewed hunger surged through him.

Turning with her on the bed, Garth lifted his head and looked down at her. Her eyes gleamed with the sparkle he had put there. There was a sheen to her flesh, and the heat of her passion cried out to be fulfilled once again. Dear God, she thought, she would never get enough of this man! Garth stroked her throat, threading his fingers through the sweat-dampened line of her hair, and he looked at her with sweet longing.

"You're incredible, Deirdre. Not just as a lover, but as a woman. I can't even imagine what it's going to be like without you."

Such an admission was more than Deirdre could bear. She laced her arms around his neck and drew him to her, just so he wouldn't see the anguish in her eyes. She wanted him to stay. She wanted him with her for the rest of her life, but she had no right to say such a thing to him. She had promised she would ask nothing of him, and she would keep that promise no matter what the cost.

Chapter Four

Deirdre glanced at the clock over the mantel. It was past midnight. She'd been sitting there for hours, half expecting to hear from Garth that evening, even though Roy hadn't told her when he would call. Garth must have kept his plans to himself, because Roy certainly would have told her when to expect the visit, and given her plenty of time to prepare herself, if he could have.

The idea of refusing to see Garth crossed Deirdre's mind, but she knew she was really too curious to pass up the chance to find out why he would come back after all this time and without prior warning. Garth wasn't the kind of man who acted on impulse. No, she thought resolutely, he must have a very definite reason for this trip. It must be something very personal, since he hadn't even told Roy. Deirdre shook her head at the thought. For all she knew, Garth might simply be in Washington on business. Maybe he had just decided to combine business with pleasure. Pleasure! Deirdre laughed to herself. She doubted Garth Logan had thought of her once in that context after they had left the cabin and come home.

After carrying the tea tray into the kitchen, Deirdre checked all the downstairs windows and doors before wearily climbing the stairs. The sailing had been as enervating as it was enjoyable. All she wanted now was a good night's sleep.

She showered in the main hall bath instead of the one between her room and Andy's. She didn't want to disturb his sleep, knowing how much he needed his rest in order to get well again.

Afterward she carried a hairbrush into his room and sat next to his bed. She watched him sleep while she brushed the tangles out of her freshly washed hair. As her fingers worked, Deirdre thought again about that night. It was easy to close her eyes and imagine Garth's hands threading through her hair as he made love to her again and again. Sleep had been the furthest thing from their minds, and they had given in to it only when necessity overpowered their desires.

Deirdre woke before Garth and saw the world very differently in the light of day. She slipped from Garth's arms without disturbing his sleep, and made herself a cup of coffee. As she sat on the end of the bed, sipping her coffee and watching him sleep, she was fully aware of the ache inside her that she knew would last a very long time. She had been a fool to think one night of loving would be enough. Perhaps with a man she wasn't so very much in love with it would be, but there was no use wishing she felt less for Garth . . . and there was no use wishing last night hadn't happened. It had, and now she could only deal with it.

She had dressed and prepared a second cup of coffee by the time Garth woke. He appeared startled when he reached out and found the bed empty, but he smiled when she came back with the coffee.

"God, I thought you were part of a dream," he murmured, his voice thick with sleep.

Deirdre forced a smile, touching her hand to his bristly jaw. "I brought you some coffee, but you'd better drink it fast. It's getting late and I imagine Craig has returned to the house by now."

A scowl appeared on his face as he took the cup from her and placed it on the table. "That can wait a while longer, can't it? Come back to bed."

Deirdre longed to yield to him, but in leaving his arms

that morning, she had made a major decision and relenting now would only mean more heartbreak later.

Sensing her reluctance, Garth asked, "Regrets, Deirdre?"

She shook her head and smiled, but she wasn't very convincing. "I guess I'm just not very good at this morning-after business. I'm sorry," she murmured quietly.

Garth placed a hand over hers. "Don't be sorry, darling. The last thing I want is for you to be blasé about last night."

She bent and placed her lips softly against his. "I'm not sorry we made love and I wouldn't want you to be, either."

Garth rubbed a strand of her hair through his fingers. "That will never happen." He paused briefly, then said, "A lot depends on the work I'm doing right now, Deirdre. It's not just what *I* want to do. It's more than just negotiating labor contracts. The experience I'm gaining there is invaluable both to myself and to countless others who'll be sent after me. But last night," he whispered softly, "there was only the two of us. Nothing else mattered. Please believe that."

Deirdre managed a small smile that warded off her tears. There would be plenty of time to cry later.

With the weather cleared up and the bay waters as smooth as silk, the return trip took little time. Deirdre had little time to dwell on the confrontation with Craig and Jasamin that was yet to come, but she felt confident that last night had mellowed Garth, even though he hadn't mentioned the subject sincc waking that morning. Perhaps he was avoiding it, Deirdre thought ruefully.

"Are you still intent on punishing Craig if anything has happened between them?" she finally asked.

Garth shot her a look that was anything but understanding. Then, suddenly, he sighed heavily. "I'll reserve judgment until I see how cooperative Craig is. That's all I can promise you now."

Deirdre bit her lower lip. "You mean, if he agrees to an annulment without making waves."

"Something like that," Garth returned rather stiffly. She suspected he resented her bringing the subject up at all.

They didn't speak again until they reached the cove. Deirdre knew they were wisely avoiding an argument, but that didn't stop her from silently questioning his stubbornness.

From the dock Deirdre could see the driveway that curved around the back of the house. She saw the car bearing the insignia of the local police even before she noticed the officer at her back door.

"Oh, God," Deirdre gasped as fear gripped her chest tightly. Something terrible had happened. She could feel it with every fiber of her being.

She was out of the boat before Garth had shut off the motor. She raced to the house, but Garth caught up with her as she reached the policeman.

"What is it? What's wrong? Is it Craig?"

The officer adjusted his hat and looked down at her. "Miss Mallory?"

"Yes, yes. I'm Deirdre Mallory. Is it Craig? Is he in some kind of trouble? Has something happened?"

Garth's arm came around her waist. "Deirdre, let the man tell us," he urged, and she knew from his hold that he, too, feared the worst.

"Could you tell me your name, sir?" the officer asked.

"I'm Garth Logan. My ward, Jasamin Grant, left school sometime Friday. I believe she was with Craig Mallory."

The officer nodded. "Miss Grant is fine, but there's been a serious accident." He looked grimly at Deirdre. "I don't know the full extent of your cousin's injuries, but he was listed as critical when the ambulance brought him in late last night. The girl was held overnight for observation and I believe she's still at the hospital with him."

The officer's careful explanation did little good; Deirdre only heard him say Craig was seriously injured. She felt numb by the time Garth put her into his car and drove her to the hospital.

Garth led her into the building and up to the floor where they'd been directed. Deirdre's eyes barely focused on the blond girl who sat alone in the waiting area. As soon as she saw Garth she was in his arms and sobbing uncontrollably.

"I'm sorry . . . I'm sorry . . . I swear it wasn't my fault. I don't even know what happened. The car skidded and . . . and another was coming at us. Oh, please, Garth," she pleaded, clinging to him, "say you aren't angry with me. I'll never run off again. I swear it!"

Garth drew the girl tightly into his arms and rested his cheek against the top of her head as he stroked her long hair. So this was Jasamin Grant, thought Deirdre dispassionately. She had the sort of beauty men thrived on. Long blond hair and blue-violet eyes that were so light they appeared almost transparent. She wore designer jeans and a shirt that hugged her figure. And she looked like an innocent lamb.

Jasamin, still in Garth's protective arms, opened her eyes to find Deirdre staring at her. The girl's arms tightened around Garth's waist.

"Try to be calm, sweetheart," Garth said quietly, cupping her face with his hands and forcing her to look up at him. Deirdre was startled by the gesture, remembering Garth's hands caressing her in much the same way. She studied Jasamin's features once again and, suddenly, a very important piece of the puzzle fell into place. The one thing Garth had failed to mention was that his seventeen-year-old ward was very much in love with him.

Deirdre's thoughts were checked instantly when she heard Garth say, "You're going to have to tell me everything that happened, Jassy. If you were in any way responsible for this accident, I have to know about it."

His tone and that single question reverberated through Deirdre's mind like an echo in a long tunnel. How could he be so unfeeling! All he cared about was this girl and whether or not she could be held legally accountable for the accident.

Jasamin started to answer Garth, but Deirdre cut her off sharply. "Where's Craig? How badly is he hurt?"

Garth looked at Deirdre as though he had suddenly remembered she was there, but her icy gaze never left the girl.

Jasamin's enormous eyes stared back at her, and she took a tentative step away from Garth. "I don't know and I don't care!" Jasamin cried. "He almost got me killed! Do you think I give a damn about—"

Before Deirdre could stop herself, she slapped Jasamin hard on the face. The silence crackled between them as the girl rubbed her cheek. Deirdre was shocked by her own action, but she was far too upset to analyze why she'd done it. She only knew she wanted to cry, for Craig and for herself, because she had realized too late that what had happened between her and Garth never should have been. Jasamin Grant was all that mattered to him. Garth made that only too obvious when he grabbed Deirdre's arm firmly as if to prevent her from striking the girl again.

"I know who you are now." Jasamin was seething. "You're Deirdre, the tyrannical bitch!" she flung at her wildly. "Craig told me all about you. He can't even have a girlfriend without your being jealous! Well, if you're so hot for him, you can have him! He's a lousy lov—"

"Jasamin, for God's sake!" Garth released Deirdre's arm and turned furiously back to his ward. He shook her soundly to silence her vicious barbs. "You're hysterical. Don't say things you'll only regret later."

A sob escaped Jasamin's throat and she was drawn immediately back into Garth's arms. His concern for the girl was etched clearly on his face, and his eyes, when they met Deirdre's, were filled with pleading. For what? she wondered. Was he asking her to feel sympathy for this fragile-looking creature, who obviously cared for no one but herself?

Deirdre looked away, unable to bear the sight of Jasamin Grant in Garth's arms. She left them alone and walked down the long corridor to the nurses' station. After identifying herself, she followed one of the nurses to a nearby room. The room was in the intensive-care unit.

"You can stay with him only a few minutes," the nurse told her. "I'll try to locate the doctor, so you can speak with him about your cousin's condition. The patient might not be coherent enough to talk, but if he is, please try not to tire him. He needs as much rest as he can get."

At least Craig is conscious, Deirdre thought gratefully as she entered the room. She would be content just to see him and touch him, just to know he was alive.

He was asleep when she entered. He was in a body cast that reached his shoulders and his dark head was swathed in bandages. There were tubes running down from his nose and needles inserted in the veins of his hands. Seeing him tore Deirdre apart inside, but she didn't cry. The impact of what had happened hadn't hit her yet, and wouldn't for some time.

His lashes fluttered when she touched his hand. Craig looked at her for only a moment, then closed his eyes tightly as if he were in intense pain. The nurse, however, had assured Deirdre that he wasn't.

"Jasamin . . . is she . . . really all right?" he asked raspily. Deirdre's heart wrenched in her chest.

"Yes, Craig, yes. She's fine. I just spoke with her. She's outside with . . . with her guardian. His name is—"

"Garth Logan," Craig supplied in a quiet and strange tone of voice. He sounded as if he knew the man well . . . and hated him with a passion.

"Yes, Craig, that's his name," Deirdre said numbly. "Darling, you should have told me about Jasamin. Garth came to the house yesterday after he found out she'd left school. He was very . . . anxious about her," she said, choosing her words carefully.

"Tell him . . . take her away. Never want to . . . see her . . . again." His words came with a tremendous effort and Deirdre touched his hand in a gesture of comfort. But Craig flinched and moved his hand away as far as he could.

"Craig, you don't have to worry about anything. Just concentrate on getting well again. We'll talk about this when you're feeling—"

"Go away," Craig whispered, a tear escaping from the corner of his eye. "Let . . . me die. Please . . . let me die."

He fell asleep almost instantly. Deirdre sat next to his bed and quietly cried. Knowing that she had spent the night in a stranger's arms while Craig was lying near death was almost more than she could bear.

When the nurse returned to end the visit, Deirdre went docilely. The doctor was in the waiting room area with Garth, but Jasamin was nowhere in sight.

"Craig is going to need a great deal of care if he's to recover," the doctor told her frankly. "As I was telling Mr. Logan, he has multiple injuries, but just how much of this is permanent, it's too early to tell. We can be grateful there was no brain damage."

Deirdre sat with her hands folded tightly in her lap. "Then he will recover?"

The doctor hesitated before nodding. "It's up to Craig, Miss Mallory. I don't need to tell you his mental state, as you've spoken with him yourself. Naturally, we'll do everything we can, but I think you should realize, we're facing weeks, months of hard work."

Deirdre gasped but could say nothing. In the weeks ahead, Deirdre would learn just what the doctor meant by "work," but for now it was enough to know that Craig would live.

When the doctor had gone, Garth moved to the bench beside Deirdre and took her hand in his. "Are you all right?" he asked. She realized then how frozen she must look. She made an effort to reassure him before pulling away and standing up. Garth stood as well and followed her to the other side of the waiting area.

"I'm sorry about Jasamin," Garth said, stopping an arm's length from her without attempting to touch her again. "She's very frightened, Deirdre. Please try to understand what a trauma all this must be for her."

Deirdre was unable to comply with his wishes. All she could think about was Craig. She couldn't care about an uninjured Jasamin—and she couldn't let herself think about Garth.

"Craig saved Jasamin's life," Garth continued. "After you left, she told me Craig covered her body with his just before the car went off an embankment. He was . . ." Garth paused, then lowered his voice. "Craig was taking her back to school, Deirdre."

Deirdre was amazed by the sudden sympathy for Craig she heard in Garth's voice. Unfortunately, as far as she was concerned, it came too late, as did Garth's admission of guilt.

"Look, Deirdre, I feel lousy for what's happened. I was obviously wrong about Craig. I'll do what I can to make it up to you both."

Deirdre closed her eyes. This was the last thing she wanted to hear. The closeness they had shared had been a sham. If it hadn't been for the accident, Garth would have already left her.

"There's nothing you can do, Garth," she said, forcing her eyes to meet his. "Please . . . just go."

Garth looked as if he'd been struck. "I'm not leaving you, Deirdre. Not like this."

Deirdre swallowed, forcing back the tears blocking her throat. "There's nothing you can do for Craig or me. There's no reason for you to stay."

And there's every reason for you to go, she added silently, spying Jasamin Grant turning the corner at the far end of the corridor. Jasamin slowed her stride when she saw Deirdre and Garth together. She knew Garth wasn't romantically involved with his seventeen-year-old ward, but she couldn't ignore the special bond between them. Their closeness went beyond the physical relationship Deirdre and Garth had shared. Although their bond was not a romantic one, Deirdre envied Jasamin because she knew she herself would never have as much with Garth Logan.

"I know how hard this must be on you, Deirdre," said Garth, lifting a hand to her shoulder. "I don't want you facing this alone. I can stay as long as you need me. I *want* to stay for you, Deirdre."

For how long? Deirdre wondered, knowing he couldn't possibly stay as long as she needed him. He meant a few days, possibly a week, but eventually he would have to leave.

Stilling her trembling hands, Deirdre said evenly, "It would be better if you just left. You . . . and Jasamin. She's your responsibility, Garth. You don't owe me or Craig anything."

"That has nothing to do with it!" Garth snapped. His hands tightened on her shoulders. "Deirdre, last night wasn't just another—"

"Stop!" she cried, pressing her hands to her ears as a violent shudder rocked her to the center of her being. "I want you to go, damn it! Get that girl out of my sight! She needs you, Garth. I don't!"

Garth had not seen Jasamin coming, and now he pulled Deirdre soundly against him. "If I thought for one minute you were serious, I think I'd beat you for that." He saw Jasamin then, as the girl stopped dead in her tracks. Even though she couldn't possibly hear what they were saying, Garth lowered his voice. "Just remember, Deirdre, Jasamin and Craig won't always be between us, and when that day comes . . ." His words died as he bent his head to hers and claimed a kiss from her startled lips. Then he was gone.

Garth caught up with Jasamin and laced an arm around her small waist as he guided her back toward the elevators. Deirdre watched as the doors closed, and only then did she feel the impact of his leaving. She stood for a long time in silence, remembering what he had told her.

Then she walked over and sat down on the bench. He had practically vowed to see her again, and, somehow, those words cushioned the loneliness she faced without him.

But as the weeks passed, Deirdre was able to put the time spent with Garth, and the vow he had made upon leaving, into the proper perspective. Garth had spoken during an emotionally charged moment, perhaps because he thought it was expected of him. Whatever the reason, Deirdre was certain that he had forgotten his promise and that, in time, she would do the same.

Roy, then, had helped Deirdre through the most difficult period in her life. In the beginning, Deirdre wasn't sure just how much Roy knew about her relationship with Garth, but he wasn't at all surprised to hear Garth was the father of the child when she finally admitted to her pregnancy.

"Garth is a decent man, Deirdre," Roy said, having taken her out that evening for a quiet dinner so they could discuss the matter thoroughly. "He'll do right by you."

Deirdre groaned audibly. "I hate that expression," she said, trying to hide her true feelings. Not that she was afraid of how Garth might react to this pregnancy; after all, in the two months since the accident she hadn't heard one word directly from Garth. Roy told her of Garth's concern for her, but it was always in the context of how she was coping with Craig's condition. His letters never contained a personal message for her, nor had she expected them to.

"Are you considering an abortion, Deirdre?" Roy asked woodenly, not letting his own opinion influence her in the least.

"No!" she cried in a shaky, barely audible voice.

"No, I didn't think so," Roy returned, covering her hand gently with his own. "We'll have to let Garth know, then."

If they hadn't been in a public place, Deirdre would

surely have burst into tears. "I can't," she whispered. "I can't force him to marry me." Her voice broke despite her good intentions. "Garth never pretended to love me, Roy," she said, trying to make him understand. "I just can't force this on him. Not after . . ." She couldn't go on. How could she possibly hope to make Roy understand the way it had been between them that night? There had been no strings then; there couldn't be now.

"There is an alternative, Deirdre," said Roy. "You and Garth could be married without his ever having to come back here. It's a simple arrangement, whereby you would become Mrs. Garth Logan through a marriage by proxy. It's perfectly legal, and it's just as binding as any marriage would be. You'll sign papers, as will Garth, and both you and his child will bear his name. The only difference is that you won't be together when you take your vows."

Deirdre could have pointed out one other very important difference: the vows that should mean so much in a marriage would be only empty words in theirs. But the child would bear his father's name. . . .

"Would Garth agree to such a marriage?" she asked.

Roy hesitated only a moment. "I'm quite sure he would, Deirdre. Garth's life isn't as uncomplicated as it may seem," he said rather strangely. It wasn't like Roy to keep anything from her concerning Garth, but she knew instinctively that now Roy was holding something back. When she was about to ask him to explain, Roy withdrew his hand from hers abruptly and said, "It's really nothing for you to concern yourself with, Deirdre. It's just that Garth has been keeping very busy since . . . well, since the accident."

Oh, yes, Deirdre thought with a twinge of bitterness, Garth's work does keep him very busy. Now that Jasamin Grant was safely back at school, and Garth had eased his guilt by writing out a check to cover Craig's medical expenses, he was free to concentrate fully on his work.

Drawing a deep breath, Deirdre said, "I'll marry him, Roy, but only if he agrees to the proxy marriage. I don't ever want to see Garth Logan again." Now she had only herself to convince of that.

Deirdre didn't ask how Roy managed to get Garth to agree to such a marriage. No doubt Garth was relieved that matters could be expedited so easily. She wouldn't allow herself to dwell on such bitter thoughts. All that mattered was that Garth had agreed and the papers were being finalized.

Less than five months later, her son was born prematurely. He looked tiny and helpless, and, in spite of the bitterness she felt toward Garth, she realized then how desperately she wanted their child to survive.

Roy came to the hospital the day Deirdre was allowed to take the baby home. They stood together at the nursery window watching the child as they waited for the doctor to release him.

"Does Garth know he has a son?" Deirdre asked without emotion.

Roy looked away uncomfortably. "Yes, Deirdre, of course he knows. I let him know right away. He said if there was anything you or the baby needed . . . just to let him know."

At that moment a door closed on the past, and, with one more layer of ice wrapped around her heart, Deirdre walked over to the nurse who held her son.

Deirdre heard voices and opened her eyes to the light of day, stunned that she'd spent the night in the chair next to Andy's bed. It was Sunday, and she heard the faint ringing of church bells in the distance.

Deirdre listened to the voices again, thinking they must be Craig's and Edith's until she heard the housekeeper say, "Imagine you coming here after all this time! I knew sure as I woke up this morning, it was going to be a grand day." Deirdre's heart began to race within her chest. "Now, mind you don't wake Andy or his mom," Edith instructed. "They both had it rough these past weeks and I'll not have you disturbing their sleep."

Garth's voice was deep and strong, sending a chill of apprehension up Deirdre's spine. Last night the thoughts of facing him again had failed to stir anything in her but memories, but now she knew it wouldn't be as easy as she had thought. "I just want to see my son, Mrs. Kirk," Garth said. As far as Deirdre was concerned, he couldn't have announced his indifference about seeing his wife more clearly.

Deirdre stood just as the door opened. Her eyes met and locked with Garth's for what seemed an eternity.

"Hello, Garth," she said softly, pushing her hair back from her face. Her brush lay on the floor, and her silken bathrobe gaped open to reveal pale pink pajamas. She drew the robe around her and secured the sash.

"Hello, Deirdre. Roy told you I was here, I suppose."

"Yes, he told me. You're looking well," she said, stunned that four years had only improved his appearance.

His eyes swept over her in a gesture that annoyed her. "I wish I could say the same for you, Deirdre."

She tightened the sash of her robe with a startled jerk and averted her eyes from his intense gaze. She turned toward Andy and saw once again that he was the image of his father. She resisted the urge to straighten his sleep-ruffled hair and turned to leave just as Andy was stirring to the sound of their voices.

"If you'll excuse me, I'd like to get dressed," Deirdre said, more stiffly than intended. "Andy hasn't been well, so perhaps you should make this visit a short one. It would be best."

Deirdre went into the bathroom as she heard Andy's awakening voice. If the stranger in his room frightened him, he didn't show it.

"Who are you?" he asked, his voice groggy from sleep.

Garth hesitated only a moment before answering. "Hello, Andy. I thought your mother might have told you I was coming to see you."

Deirdre listened to no more, turning the sink tap on full

blast. She washed her face and cleaned her teeth before going into her own room.

Why she reached for a skirt and sweater rather than a pair of traditional jeans and T-shirt, she couldn't say. Certainly not to impress Garth, who'd yet to see her respectably clad.

Still, she enjoyed the feel of the soft cashmere against her skin and liked the way the pale green of the sweater reflected her eyes. It bloused over her gray-green knee-length skirt. She pulled her hair back with tortoiseshell combs that made her appear less than glamorous, but not quite schoolmarmish all the same. The last thing she wanted was for Garth to think she gave a damn what he thought of her appearance.

For good measure, she settled for a light lipstick and nothing more. The sun she had gotten the day before had heightened her features attractively and she needed nothing else.

Deirdre returned to Andy's room to find Garth sitting on the bed. "Just lie still, Andy," Garth told him in gentle tones as he worked the buttons of Andy's pajama top.

Deirdre stared in confusion until she saw how blanched her son's face was. His fevered eyes darted to her and drew her closer to the bed. She extended a hand to his forehead as Garth examined his stomach. "Andy, honey, is something—"

Andy cut her off with a cry of pain. Garth's hands lifted just as Deirdre realized what was wrong.

"Oh, God!" Deirdre exclaimed in a barely audible whisper. Garth looked at her with deep concern in his eyes.

"Your mom and I are going to take you to the hospital, Andy," Garth told him. He spoke calmly for Andy's sake, but his words hit Deirdre like a ton of bricks. Andy looked terrified and searched Deirdre's eyes for reassurance.

"It's all right, darling," she said softly, but inside she felt like a mass of quivering jelly.

Garth took the blanket from the end of the bed and tucked it around Andy before bending to scoop him up into his arms. "You trust me don't you, son?" Garth asked, smiling down at the boy.

Of course he does, Deirdre wanted to shout. He thinks you're the greatest man who ever walked the face of the earth.

"Will you make it stop hurting?" Andy asked.

"I promise," Garth assured him as he carried him through the door Deirdre had opened.

Garth placed Andy on her lap as soon as she was seated in his rented car. A worried Edith had followed them from the house and now stood at the end of the walk, looking on the verge of tears.

Deirdre could offer no reassurances and she didn't try. It was all happening so fast, she couldn't sort out the jumble of emotions that churned inside her. How could I not have known? she cried silently. Why did it have to come to this?

"It hurts, Mommy," Andy complained, trying to free his small arm from the confining blanket. Deirdre hadn't taken the time to get a light jacket, but the adrenaline pumping through her veins provided all the warmth she needed.

"Where does it hurt, Andy?" she asked, trying not to think of all the horror stories concerning appendicitis in its acute stage.

"In my tummy, where I told you before." Andy sounded impatient, but his small voice was nothing compared to the look Garth shot her. He blamed her for this, she thought. He must think she had simply ignored Andy's complaints.

"It won't be long before we reach the hospital, Andy," she said, pressing a kiss to his forehead.

"Am I going to die?" he asked, gazing at her with innocent eyes.

Deirdre trembled and began to rock him. "Don't say such things, Andy," she said, noting the whiteness of Garth's knuckles as he clutched the steering wheel.

Deirdre didn't think they would ever reach the hospital. While Andy's quiet moans of pain made the trip hard enough, Garth's damnable looks of accusation made it unbearable. He had no right to behave this way, after ignoring his son's existence for three years, but that hardly mattered now.

Finally, they reached the emergency-room entrance. Leaving the car running, Garth climbed out and came around to take Andy from Deirdre's lap.

"Find a parking space," he ordered. "I'll meet you inside."

He was gone before she had a chance to object, and Deirdre was forced to comply with his demands. But the car was bigger than her own small one, and maneuvering it was quite difficult. She killed the engine three times and nearly scraped another car before she finally got it parked and hurried to the emergency room.

Garth and her son were nowhere in sight. Deirdre walked over to the information window. "My son was just brought in. Can you tell me where they took him?"

"Andrew Logan?" the woman asked, checking the papers before her.

"Yes, that's his name. Is he being examined?" she asked.

"He's being prepared for surgery, Mrs. Logan. Your husband said you could give us the information we need, since he's with the boy." The nurse handed Deirdre an assortment of forms that made her senses whirl. I should be with my son, she screamed silently, not some damned father who had just reappeared!

"Can't this wait?" she cried to the nurse.

The woman smiled understandingly. "It's really vital, Mrs. Logan. It won't take more than a few minutes."

But parking the car already took me fifteen minutes, she thought angrily. And in that short period of time, the care of her child had been taken from her hands. Did Garth really think she wouldn't have brought Andy to the hospital if he hadn't been there?

Deirdre concentrated on filling out the forms and, twenty minutes later, handed them back to the woman behind the desk. "Has Dr. Foggarty selected a surgeon yet?" Deirdre asked. Even though Garth wouldn't have known to ask for the family physician, Deirdre was certain Edith would have phoned him the moment they left the house. He was probably with Andy at that very moment.

"Dr. Foggarty?" The nurse looked confused. "I can call him if you want, Mrs. Logan, but your husband specifically requested that a pediatric surgeon be called in. Dr. Peterson is with your son now."

Dr. Peterson was the complete opposite of the elderly, trustworthy Dr. Foggarty. He looked barely old enough to be out of medical school, Deirdre thought critically. But she knew such thoughts were as unreasonable as the competitiveness she felt with Andy's father. Nothing should matter but getting her son well. Nothing!

"There isn't much I can tell you right now, Mr. Logan," the young doctor said. Deirdre had just found Garth and the doctor, but they were both ignoring her presence. "I'm sure you did the right thing by bringing the boy in now. Your actions might very well have saved your son's life. I'll speak with you again when we're finished."

"Please, I want to see my son," Deirdre interjected.

Dr. Peterson shook his head. "I'm sorry, but he's already in the operating room. Try to relax, Mrs. Logan."

As soon as the doors closed, Garth spun on her angrily. "Your housekeeper told me Andy has been sick for three weeks now. When the hell were you going to do something about it, Deirdre? When you woke up some morning and found him dead?"

Deirdre's eyes widened incredulously. "For your information, Andy has seen a doctor, just as he sees a doctor every time he gets sick. Not that I consider that any concern of yours!" she blurted out furiously.

Garth's brows furrowed deeply. "He's my son, too, Deirdre," he said. "Contrary to what you may believe, I do care very much about my son."

Deirdre had every reason to challenge such a statement, but something kept her from doing so. Whether he'd given Andy a second thought all these years or not seemed unimportant at that moment. What did matter was that his worry for his son now was very real . . . very intense.

Deirdre averted her challenging eyes and said, "Andy has never been a strong child. I was going to call a specialist tomorrow if Andy hadn't improved."

With a heavy sigh, Garth raked his hands through his hair. "I'm sorry. I shouldn't have said what I did. I just . . . didn't expect this to happen."

Deirdre didn't know what to say to him, so she opted for silence. She walked over and sat down on a low bench, prepared to wait just as she had waited four years earlier. They kept a silent vigil for what seemed like hours. Occasionally Garth would press a Styrofoam cup of coffee into her hand, but it was merely to replace the one she'd let get cold.

After what seemed an eternity, Dr. Peterson returned. He sighed heavily and smiled at Garth and Deirdre, who stood side by side.

"We were lucky," he told them. "A few more hours and we might not have been. It will be some time before he's awake. Why don't you get something to eat and come back in an hour or so?"

Garth extended a hand and smiled brightly. "Thank you, Doctor. We will."

Dr. Peterson looked at Deidre. "Are you all right, Mrs. Logan?"

Deirdre had gotten very good at guarding her true emotions, and she used her ability now. She nodded and smiled, but that was all.

After the doctor had gone, Garth turned to face her. He studied her curiously, as though he expected her to break down at any moment. "Let's take his advice and get some breakfast," he said. When Deirdre agreed, he pressed his hand against the center of her back and guided her toward the elevators.

Chapter Five

The hospital had three dining facilities. The cafeteria was filled with employees on their coffee break, and the adjoining canteen was quite popular with the lunch crowd who didn't mind sandwiches popped into a microwave. Garth and Deirdre opted for the semielegant coffee shop, which was designed for visitors seeking a little peace and quiet. Because the coffee shop was empty, the young girl in a pert gold waitress uniform came over to their table promptly.

"Are you still serving breakfast?" Garth asked, discarding the luncheon menu that sat on the table's edge.

"I can bring you something from the cafeteria," the girl replied accommodatingly.

"Good. What will you have, Deirdre?" he asked.

"Oh, toast and coffee will be fine," she replied wearily.

Garth frowned. "Scrambled eggs, bacon, toast, and a fruit cup if you have it, please. And my wife will have the same."

Deirdre darted a sharp look at him, but the waitress' smile kept her from saying anything. Obviously the young girl found Deirdre in a very enviable position.

Deirdre wasn't surprised by this. Garth was still the most compellingly attractive man she'd ever seen. His dark eyes still had that piercing quality that reached her at the core of her being. Once, she had found his intense gaze quite appealing, but now she could think only of the disadvantage it put her at. Not that she still loved him, but she couldn't deny that his presence had a curious effect on her.

The pale blue shirt he wore under his dark, casual suit was opened at the throat for comfort. A matting of light brown hair appeared at the deepest plunge of his shirt opening, teasing her eyes to explore further. A stab of memory shot through Deirdre. The primitive sexuality of their lovemaking returned to haunt her just as it had the night before. She knew if she'd dared to close her eyes the memory would overwhelm her.

But Deirdre wouldn't allow that to happen. She had her feet planted firmly on the ground, and she would never again allow herself to appear vulnerable. Not to Garth—not to any man.

"I gather Craig is still living with you," Garth said, cutting into her thoughts.

Deirdre frowned at his disapproving tone. "Yes, of course," she said, meeting his level gaze.

Garth's brow lifted. "Of course." It was a flat statement. "How is he?"

"Craig is fine," she lied. "Just fine. You're looking well, Garth," she said hastily, knowing any discussion of Craig would inevitably bring up the past, and she wanted to avoid that at all costs.

"So you said," he reminded her. "And in my own charming way, I said that you did not. You're thinner than I remember, but still quite beautiful."

The waitress brought the coffee and didn't miss hearing the last remark. She nearly purred.

Deirdre's hand encircled her cup when the waitress had gone again. "I've been keeping busy at work," she told him. "And it's more fashionable to be slim these days."

"You own your own dress shop now," Garth said.

"You should know," said Deirdre quietly. "You paid for it."

"I thought it was what you wanted. You did tell me you had hopes of owning it someday, and since you insisted on working after Andy was born . . ." Garth spread his hands. "I hoped it would please you, Deirdre."

"Yes, it did," she said hastily. "Thank you."

Her politeness clearly annoyed him. But what did he expect her reaction to be? she wondered. She hadn't wanted such a generous gift, especially since he had responded so indifferently to the news of Andy's birth. *"If you or the boy need anything, just let him know."* That was the only message he had sent. As long as she lived, Deirdre would never forget how devastated those words had made her feel.

"You haven't asked why I'm here, Deirdre. Aren't you the least bit curious?" Garth had been studying her closely.

"I assume your visit has to do with business of some kind. Roy didn't say for sure. I don't think he knew why."

"He knows now," Garth snapped. "I saw him this morning, before I came to see you. I wanted to make sure of a few things myself before asking you about it."

"I don't understand," Deirdre said, twin creases forming between her brows.

Garth's gaze was challenging. "I think you do, Deirdre. Roy is the one, isn't he? He's the man you're involved with. The reason you've suddenly decided you want your freedom."

Ice water thrown in her face couldn't have shocked Deirdre more. Her mouth opened mechanically, but no words came out.

"I'll tell you the same thing I told him, Deirdre." Garth leaned toward her for emphasis. "Our marriage might not be a conventional one, but we do have a child and there is no way in hell I'll ever divorce you unless I'm sure it's in Andy's best interests."

Deirdre felt her nails biting into the palms of her hands. "I can't believe this!" she cried, but it was barely an audible whisper. "I'm not involved with Roy! He happens to be married!"

Garth stared icily, clearly doubting her word. "Yes, and

he's legally separated from his wife, while you have never lived with your husband. Makes things very cozy, doesn't it?" he sneered.

Deirdre's green eyes sparkled with anger. "How dare you accuse me of such a thing! How dare you!"

But Garth was undaunted. He smiled and ran the tip of his tongue over his upper lip, thoroughly pleased with himself.

"That's what I came to see, Deirdre. Those fabulously expressive green eyes. Your soul is in them, sweet witch. And your soul, as you well know, belongs to me."

"You make it sound like I sold it to the devil."

He winked with confidence. "Not sold it, my darling. Gave it, and I intend to keep it until I am truly sated."

Deirdre ate little of her breakfast. Between the gallons of coffee she had consumed, and Garth, she didn't have much of an appetite.

Garth ate heartily, but, then, the victors always did, she mused bitterly. She had no idea why he thought she wanted her freedom, but she couldn't deny it until she found out what was behind the accusation. The only thing she knew surely was that Roy Carlysle had something to do with it. Why else had he been so ill at ease when he told her Garth was in town? Roy had done or said something to bring Garth back here, and she was determined to hold her tongue until she found out what it was.

"Excuse me, are you the Logans?" the waitress asked. Garth acknowledged this and she added, "They just called down. Your son is awake and he's asking for his mother."

Deirdre's relief was so vast, she momentarily forgot Garth's accusations and flashed him a brilliant smile, which he returned. Whatever her personal feelings about Garth's return, Deirdre knew she couldn't doubt the sincerity of his feelings for his son. The question was, why did it take something like this to make her realize how much he cared? Garth might have never made an effort to contact his son, but he did marry her and give Andy his name. Whatever else Deirdre felt for him, she had to be grateful for that.

With the strange nurse hovering over him, Andy looked small and frightened. He was in a recovery room lined with beds, but the others were empty. His cheeks were wet from crying and, when he saw his mother, a small hand brushed the tears away.

"Where were you, Mommy?" he asked, blaming her for his fright, as any child might.

Deirdre drew the blanket over him and bent to kiss his cheek. "I was downstairs having breakfast with your . . . with your daddy." Garth couldn't have missed her hesitation, but he didn't comment on it. "I'm here with you now, so you needn't be afraid."

"Is that man really my daddy?" His eyes moved behind Deirdre to Garth.

Deirdre's heart wrenched. "Yes, and he's come a very long way to be with you, too, so you'd better be on your best behavior," she teased playfully.

"Or he won't like me, right?" Andy queried.

Deirdre frowned. "What a silly thing to say."

"Well, Craig doesn't like me when I'm bad. He won't read to me or even play games with me."

Garth moved closer to the bed, placing a hand on Deirdre's shoulder and making her extremely uncomfortable. He placed his other hand over hers and Andy's. Under other circumstances, the whole scene would have been quite touching, Deirdre thought ruefully.

"I'll always like you, Tiger," said Garth softly. "Good or bad, you'll always be my son."

Garth moved his hand again and traced the gold band Deirdre wore on her finger. He bore no such signs of their proxy marriage, and she didn't doubt he was wondering why she did. When she moved away uncomfortably, her eyes happened to meet his and her doubts faded swiftly. He was pleased that she wore a wedding band, even though Roy had placed it on her finger.

"If you want to stay with Andy, I'll go and see about

his room accommodations," Garth suggested, and turned to walk away.

Deirdre thought the children's ward would be perfectly acceptable, but she suspected Garth wanted a private room for his son and she didn't want to make a scene in front of Andy.

Much to Deirdre's relief, Andy was soon moved to a four-unit room where only two of the other beds were occupied. The other children were about a year older than Andy and, if it weren't for the cast one wore and the inability to talk the other suffered from because of a recent tonsillectomy, Deirdre wouldn't have thought either was sick at all. The cheeriness of the room's decor and the sight of the other boys pleased Andy as well.

"Andy might be here for as long as a week," Garth told her quietly while the nurse was settling him into the bed. "I thought he might like the company of other children."

"He would," Deirdre agreed. "Thank you for being so thoughtful."

Garth's expression was unreadable. "He's my son, Deirdre. What else should I be?"

"I only meant—"

"I know what you meant," he snapped. "I wonder if other wives find it necessary to thank their children's fathers as often as you do."

Rather than draw the attention of the nurses and other parents in the room, Deirdre fell silent. Garth, however, did not feel the same inhibition, as he continually criticized her about one thing or another: her thinness, Andy's illness, and now her politeness toward him. Garth wasn't going to make this easy for her, even though he must know how much she resented his sudden return and unfounded accusations.

As the afternoon progressed, Deirdre met the parents of the other boys in the room. She liked the Douglases very much and found their son Nicky enchanting, in spite of the discomfort his broken leg caused him. The Hansens were a bit older and had obviously been through this before with other children. Deirdre found herself following their lead in entertaining her bedridden son.

Garth had come and gone throughout the afternoon, disappearing finally at four. By six Deirdre began to wonder if he had left for the day. He hadn't mentioned his plans, but with the others around, such explanations were difficult.

But just as Deirdre decided that she had seen the last of Garth for the day, the door opened and an enormous stuffed panda appeared in the room. It was so big, she couldn't see the person behind it until one ear was bent down and Garth's head appeared.

"Daddy!" cried Andy, giggling with delight. By now Deirdre had gotten used to hearing that word.

"Where on earth did you find such a thing?" Deirdre asked. "And on Sunday!"

Depositing the beast at the side of the bed, Garth replied, "I have my sources." He smiled at Andy. "What do you think of our new friend, Andy? I call him Pandy after you, or do you prefer Pandrew?"

Andy giggled again and the other boys chimed in with their more worldly suggestions. "Pandora!" shouted Nicky Douglas, and everyone groaned when Nicky's father suggested Panocchio. It came down to a vote between Andy's own choice of Pancake and Deirdre's Peter Panda. Deirdre's suggestion won, but she had a suspicion Pancake had stolen Andy's heart and would be the name that stuck, even if only in Andy's mind.

"Peter Panda is going to keep you company tonight while your mommy goes home and gets some rest," Garth announced with sly proficiency.

"Oh, no, I'd rather stay," Deirdre blurted out, undoing all of Garth's painstaking psychological techniques.

Andy was instantly alert. "I want Mommy to stay!" he said firmly.

Garth drew a deep breath for patience. "Be reasonable,

Andy. Your mother has been here all day and she's tired. She'll see you again in the morning."

"No!" cried the boy stubbornly. "Please don't go, Mommy!"

Deirdre put her arms around him. "He's only a baby, Garth. Please don't make an issue of this."

"I'm not a baby!" Andy argued with vehemence, but his small hands refused to let her go.

"No, of course you're not, darling. You're a very big boy," Deirdre returned, feeling torn between father and son, even though she'd stupidly caused this all herself.

"You said I was a baby," Andy pouted stubbornly.

"Well, I didn't mean it like that! Just be quiet now, Andy," she said authoritatively. "You shouldn't get upset."

After a while she was able to quiet Andy enough to be able to move away from him. "I'll be back in a minute, darling. Just lie quietly and I'll see about getting you a book to read before bedtime."

Garth followed her from the room. The corridor was empty, giving her a chance to speak freely.

"Andy can be very stubborn when he wants to be."

"You mean bratty, don't you?" Garth flung at her.

Deirdre's lips compressed tightly for a moment, but the anger passed. "All right, yes! But I know how upset he'll be if I leave him. He can make himself quite sick and I don't think that would be good for him at this time."

Garth was unyielding, but he didn't really know his son, did he, Deirdre thought caustically. "Do you expect to keep a bedside vigil for the entire week, Deirdre?"

"No, of course not! Tomorrow I'll see if Craig can spare some time to come and sit with him for a few hours."

"Craig!" Garth exclaimed, his mouth twisting angrily. His hands gripped her upper arms and he pressed her back into the cold, stone wall. "I suppose I should be pleased you didn't suggest Roy! Get this straight, Deirdre! That boy is mine. Mine! And as long as I'm able, I'll be the one to see to his needs. And that includes filling in the hours you can't be here with him."

"You can't just bulldoze your way into our lives, Garth." She breathed unsteadily, much too aware of the closeness of their bodies. As if sensing her awareness, Garth moved his hands over her shoulders to cup the sides of her neck, causing her pulse to leap erratically. Deirdre tried pulling away, but it only gave him reason to move closer and press his thighs into hers boldly. Garth's lips were inches from hers when she cried, "Garth, for God's sake, we're in a hospital!"

But he didn't yield. "Then stop provoking me by saying such rash things," he breathed huskily. "You are my wife and Andy is my son." He forced her eyes to lift to his by pressing his thumbs gently along her jawline. "I don't have to bulldoze my way into your lives. I am very much a part of them already. Deny it if you will, but Andy is proof enough for me."

In spite of the vulnerable position she was in, Deirdre's pride surged and she said, "Andy is your son, but that's all."

"If I thought for one minute you loved Roy, I wouldn't question a divorce, but I know you, Deirdre. Roy Carlysle could never satisfy you the way I did," he declared with arrogant pride.

"Garth, please!" Deirdre cried in a whisper, lifting her hands to force him away, knowing that if she didn't his lips would be on hers in seconds. But it wasn't her strength, or even her plea, that caused him to release her. The door opened and the Douglases came out. Their smiles were spontaneous.

"Don't worry so much about Andy," Mrs. Douglas told Deirdre. "The first night is always rough. More so on the parents."

Deirdre knew the woman had misread her expression, but better she should believe Deirdre was upset because of Andy than admit that the closeness to Garth had upset her.

Deirdre managed a smile. "Yes, I'm sure you're right. Thank you."

"Why don't you join us for dinner, Garth," suggested Mr. Douglas thoughtfully. "Sure beats going home alone," he said, winking teasingly at Deirdre. If only they knew, thought Deirdre.

But was he alone? she wondered, surveying Garth's composed smile. He hadn't mentioned Jasamin all day, but that didn't mean she wasn't still with him, as Deirdre knew she had been for the past three years.

"Thanks, but I have some business to take care of tonight. Perhaps we can make it another time."

The man smiled and slipped an arm around his wife's waist. "Sure, anytime. Take it easy, Deirdre."

Deirdre watched as they walked away, envying their obvious closeness and contentment. Strange, how she hadn't really noticed other couples before.

"You should have gone with them," Deirdre said wearily. "They seem very nice."

"They may be," Garth agreed, "but I meant what I said. I do have business to attend to, and I have an engagement for dinner."

"A business dinner?" Deirdre asked curiously.

"Not exactly. Partly business, but mostly personal."

"Is Jasamin with you?" The question slipped out before she could stop herself.

"Why would you think that?"

Deirdre shrugged and glanced down the corridor as a nurse rounded the corner. "No reason. You are still her guardian, aren't you? Technically, that is."

"For a few months yet. She isn't quite twenty-one."

Deirdre's eyes moved back to him. "You haven't answered my question. Is she with you?"

"Would it bother you if she were?"

Deirdre bit her lip. His elusiveness angered her unreasonably.

"No, it wouldn't bother me." Her reply was bland and left room for doubt. But she was thinking of Craig. If she could spare him the pain of seeing Jasamin again, she would. Any reminder of that girl was still hard for him to deal with.

"I'm glad that it wouldn't bother you, Deirdre," Garth said, then turned and strode down the corridor.

Deirdre watched him walk away. Garth apparently smiled at the nurse walking by, for once he was past, the young woman turned for a second look. The curious smile was still on her face by the time she reached Deirdre. Garth didn't look back.

Chapter Six

The faraway cry of the telephone stirred Deirdre to wakefulness. Turning from her back to her side, she stretched her arms in an arc overhead. She woke refreshed; she was getting used to the catnaps and would probably never need another full night's sleep again.

The sun was streaming through the windows and Deirdre looked at it as if she'd never noticed it before. Then she realized why. It should be at least four o'clock in the afternoon, but then why was the morning sun lighting her eastern window so brightly?

Deirdre bolted upright in bed and reached for her alarm clock. The pin was pressed down and the clock read nine-fifteen.

"What on earth!" she cried in confusion, knowing she'd set the clock when she came home after Andy had had his lunch at eleven-thirty.

For a moment Deirdre thought she must be dreaming, but then the door opened and Edith's head peeked in.

"Oh, dear, I was afraid that darned phone would wake you. It was just that girl Sally from the store. Nothing urgent," she assured her. "She just wanted you to know she didn't make it to the bank in time to make the deposit last night, so she locked everything up in the safe in your office. She opened at the regular time this morning," Edith concluded with a nod of satisfaction.

"Edith, how long have I been sleeping?" Deirdre demanded.

The woman shuffled guiltily. "Round the clock, I'd say.

Now, don't look at me with those big green eyes. If you want to blame somebody, you can blame that husband of yours. It was his idea to shut the alarm off after you'd gone to sleep. Can't say it was such a bad idea, though. You haven't budged since yesterday afternoon."

That made it Friday, Deirdre realized, shaking the grogginess out of her head. She supposed she should be thankful Garth was there to take over, but her pride got in the way. After all, she'd seen Garth only in passing all week, and they never exchanged more than civilities for Andy's benefit. Garth always used business as an excuse to leave the hospital once she was there to take over, and, as he never returned until the next morning to relieve her, Deirdre could only assume he was as anxious to avoid her as she was him.

Andy, however, was another story. The novelty of having his father home hadn't even begun to wear off, and his probing questions became more and more difficult to answer.

"Garth said Dr. Peterson might let Andy come home today," Edith said, cutting into her thoughts. "It sure was a golden day when that man of yours turned up. I look forward to having him around the house. Andy could use a strong male influence like his dad."

Deirdre looked sharply at her. "Craig provides an acceptable male influence as far as I'm concerned."

Edith was undaunted. "Craig has his own problems to deal with. You mark my words. That man is going to be good for this household. A boy needs his dad, and he's lucky to have one that loves him as much as Garth does. Come to think of it," she said smartly, clicking her tongue while she eyed Deirdre, "you could use a bit of manhandlin' yourself!"

Deirdre tied the sash of her robe tightly, but looking into the cheval mirror, she wished she hadn't. She could see how thin she was getting.

She lifted a hand to her face. "Somehow I can't see a man wanting to handle me. God, I look awful."

Edith chuckled. "Just a mite thin. I'll fix you a big breakfast and leave it on the stove. I want to get that room spick and span for you and your husband. He sent his things over from the hotel early this morning," she announced quite casually.

The full impact of Edith's words didn't hit Deirdre for a minute. As Edith left the room Deirdre gazed after her dazedly. Suddenly she gasped and brought a hand to her forehead. Garth was moving in!

Obviously Edith had accepted this without question, but Deirdre never would. She knew this wasn't a spur-of-the-moment decision on his part. He had planned this all along, and he fully expected her to stand by and let it happen.

Deirdre spun away from the mirror, not liking what she saw there. Her eyes were shining with a brightness that had nothing to do with her long sleep. The brilliance in her eyes was born of anticipation of what was to come with Garth living under the same roof. While he had intimated no sexual interest in her in the past week, he had made it clear on the first morning that he considered her very much his wife. He couldn't have chosen a more provocative way to prove his point.

"No!" Deirdre cried aloud. "I can't let that happen. I can't let him move in here!"

She left the room and raced down the hall to where the doors of the master bedroom were slid back into their casings. No one had slept in that room since before Deirdre's mother had died. As a semiinvalid, she'd preferred a room on the lower floor and her father had converted an adjoining dressing room into a small bedroom for himself. Even after her mother had died, he hadn't returned to the master bedroom, where five generations of Mallorys had been conceived.

The room had been closed off for years, entered only for infrequent cleanings. But now the French doors on either side of the bed were thrown wide, airing the room for occupancy.

New lace curtains hung in hourglass fashion on the French doors, and on the large four-poster bed lay a hand-worked comforter of cream satin that Deirdre's mother had made.

Deirdre was running a hand over the rosewood armoire when she heard a sound from the doorway. Turning, she heard Craig say, "He makes himself right at home, doesn't he?"

"I didn't invite him to move in, Craig," Deirdre responded flatly. "And I can assure you, I don't want him here any more than you do."

"But you won't do anything to stop him, will you?" Craig said challengingly. "You don't owe him anything, Deirdre," he went on, not giving her a chance to respond. "He hasn't given you a thought in four years. Not even when you had his kid," he sneered.

The shock of Garth's plans for moving in had worn off, and with it, so had all Deirdre's rational objections.

"He is Andy's father," Deirdre reminded Craig, wondering what made his bitterness so all-consuming.

Craig's mouth twisted sardonically. "I'm sure he'll use that fact to his advantage sooner or later. You're married to a piece of paper, not a man who happens to have fathered your child. A piece of paper that wouldn't even exist if it weren't for Andy. Try to remember that when you're sharing that bed with him, Deirdre."

Her eyes widened. "I'm not going to sleep with him," she bit out harshly. She knew what he had said was true, but the last thing she needed was to be reminded of it continually. Garth's presence did that.

Craig's laugh was cynical. "Of course you will. If he wants you to, that is. I suppose he feels he's paid enough for the privilege."

Craig had always resented Garth's paying his medical bills, but that was just the tip of the iceberg. Craig truly despised Garth, but why, Deirdre didn't know.

She raked a hand through her thick copper hair. She had learned to live with Craig's moods, and had done her best to shelter Andy from him when his bitterness drove him to drink. Craig had never been a violent person, but sometimes Deirdre wished he would explode occasionally, rather than keep everything knotted up inside him.

Knowing that an argument would only make matters worse, Deirdre turned toward Craig and said, "I thought you had some sails to repair before the weekend." Craig enjoyed working on the boats, but he was indifferent to the praise he received from the owners. Money was reward enough, and money was all Craig seemed to care about. Money, and sometimes Andy. If she and Craig had ever been truly close, the discovery that she carried Garth Logan's child after knowing him less than a day had destroyed that closeness. Just as it had intensified his resentment of Garth.

"I'm almost finished," Craig said. "I thought I could use a break, but I can see I was wasting my time. You're a fool to trust him, Deirdre," he flung over his shoulder as he left the room.

Deirdre returned to her own room to shower and change before returning to the hospital. She didn't want Garth living in their home any more than Craig did, but she had to think of Andy. In spite of her feelings for Garth, she could never destroy Andy's newfound feeling for his father. When she realized Andy had been building an image of his father that was greater than life, Deirdre had done nothing to destroy it. Perhaps because she had once loved Garth and her son deserved to know he was a product of that love. Whatever the reason, if Garth left again soon, she would go on pretending he was the greatest father in the world. She'd do it for Andy's sake.

After her shower Deirdre dressed in slacks out of habit. She had found herself in less than comfortable positions on that tiny lounge bench in Andy's room.

Today she pulled on cotton ducks of bottle green and an overshirt of green blends. A twisted rope belt at the waist smoothed the lines to a stylish fashion and the braiding matched the rope sandals on her feet.

She drove her own small car, having adamantly refused to drive Garth's after that first day. He had found this amusing, but didn't insist that she get used to it.

Deirdre arrived at the hospital expecting Andy to be overjoyed to see her, or perhaps pouting because she hadn't been there last night. What she found was anything but.

The tonsillectomy was gone, but Nicky Douglas would remain for yet another week. But the other beds were filled, or at least they would have been if everyone in the room hadn't been gathered around Nicky's bed to watch Garth's magic show. At least twenty children, brought in by the aides, also stood watching. Deirdre smiled at the children, whose eyes were bright with wonder as quarters began appearing from the most unexpected places. Not surprisingly, cries of "Do more, do more" rang out with the applause.

Garth caught sight of Deirdre and a mischievous smile touched his mouth. "One more," he promised, crossing the room toward her. "But for this, I'll need a beautiful lady assistant. Ah . . . good, a volunteer," he said, taking her hand and guiding her toward the assembled group.

"Are you going to make Mommy disappear?" Andy said, with evident delight at the prospect.

"Andy!" Deirdre scolded mildly.

Garth laughed and turned to face the audience. "I can make this lady turn any color you children would like. Just name it," he said with a curious air of confidence.

A slew of ideas followed, much to Deirdre's chagrin, but finally, Garth's hand lifted for silence.

"Red it is," he announced, and promptly drew Deirdre into his arms and kissed her soundly on the mouth.

A roar of laughter achieved the promised results and Deirdre brought her hands to her heated cheeks.

"Hey, it worked!" cried Nicky Douglas, and by then everyone was laughing with delight. The children would have begged for more but the aides were already beginning to shuffle them back to their various rooms.

"Is there no limit to your talents?" Deirdre asked, unable to muster up any anger about having been used so blatantly.

Garth smiled with pride. "Just making use of a golden opportunity to kiss my very beautiful wife. Would you have allowed it otherwise?" he asked boldly.

Deirdre was at a loss for a clever answer, so she turned her attention immediately to her son.

"Dr. Peterson is going to let me go home today," Andy announced cheerfully.

"He said maybe, Andy," Garth interjected firmly.

"But you promised!" Andy said defiantly.

"I did no such thing, and stop behaving like a spoiled brat." Garth's tone was harsh, but Andy, who would have otherwise pouted for hours, recovered almost instantly.

"Craig sends his love, darling," Deirdre told him, hoping to relieve the tension she suddenly felt. That kiss may have been a trick, but she felt the magic of it through to her bones.

"Why didn't Craig come and see me? I asked you to see if he would," Andy reminded her petulantly.

"I know you did, Andy, but you know how busy Craig is this time of year. Besides, they only let mommies and daddies visit," she said, hoping the excuse would satisfy him.

Andy appeared defiant. "Uncle Roy came to see me last night."

This surprised Deirdre, as she hadn't heard from Roy herself all week. But she realized Andy's words startled Garth for a different reason; in light of their present situation, "Uncle Roy" did not sit well with Andy's possessive father.

"That was very nice of Mr. Carlysle," she corrected with caution. Uncle Roy, indeed! Even she didn't approve and had no idea Andy had taken to calling him that. Had Roy encouraged it? she wondered.

"He brought me some Dr. Seuss books and he said he was real sorry he missed you and Daddy. I told him

Daddy went with Nicky's mom and daddy to have dinner. I stayed all by myself like a big boy," he announced proudly.

Dr. Peterson's arrival brought the topic of Roy Carlysle to an immediate halt. He smiled at Deirdre. "Well, Mrs. Logan, it looks like your husband finally convinced you to get some rest."

Deirdre shot Garth a look, but he was still too grim over Andy's words to notice. "Yes, he did," she admitted with a smile.

"I suggest you two grab a cup of coffee while I check over my needlepoint. If Andy hasn't busted his stitches by laughing so much, you can probably take him home today."

Upon those words, Andy was glad to be left alone with the doctor. Deirdre and Garth walked outside to the waiting area, both deciding against a cup of coffee from the machine.

She didn't give him a chance to attack her about Andy's familiarity with Roy. "I understand you're moving into my house," she said in a brittle, accusing tone. She would wait to find out precisely what his intentions were before committing herself one way or the other.

The corners of his mouth curved upward. "Do you have any objections that make sense, or are you just being obstinate?"

"I think you could have at least asked," she returned.

Garth settled onto the bench with a sigh of frustration and weariness, as if he thought the whole discussion was unnecessary. "Is that really what's bugging you, Deirdre? Or is it what Craig's going to think that's worrying you?"

Deirdre's lashes fluttered. "Craig . . . has nothing to do with this," she said defensively, but she knew she wasn't fooling Garth for a second.

"I think Craig has everything to do with this objection of yours," Garth argued, his voice thick with derision. Then, suddenly, the lines of his face set, and his eyes searched the depths of hers. "What about you, Deirdre? How do *you* feel?"

Deirdre had dreaded such a direct question, but she lifted her chin proudly. "I don't like the idea one bit, Garth. I don't trust your motives. Not for moving into my house, nor for coming back here in the first place." She didn't really believe Garth had come all the way back just to find out if she and Roy were having an affair. What could Roy have told him, she wondered, that would lead him to believe she wanted her freedom?

Garth's regard was critically assessing. "Did you really think I would let you divorce me without a fight, Deirdre? Our marriage might be nothing more than a document, but our son is a very real product of something very beautiful . . . very special that happened between us. You can't deny that, Deirdre. And you can't deny me the right to know my son."

Drawing on her inner reserve of strength, Deirdre returned his intense gaze with frozen features. Whether I want my freedom from you or not, she thought, I can't let you back into my life, Garth. There's no place for you there.

"I won't deny you the right to know your son," she echoed coolly. "Just as long as you understand, that's the only right you're entitled to."

Garth frowned, then smiled derisively. "Deirdre, my love, you're far too mistrusting. I'll admit the thought of sleeping with you again is not unappealing, but, while I do have certain conjugal rights, I'm not so desperate for a woman that I would force my own wife into sharing my bed."

Deirdre's eyes narrowed. "Just so long as we understand one another." She looked impatiently at her watch, wishing the doctor would hurry with his examination. She was as anxious to end this conversation with Garth as she was to take her son home.

"There's one other thing I haven't mentioned,

Deirdre," said Garth offhandedly. "Jasamin will be here in a couple of days."

Deirdre's eyes widened in astonishment as her reserve crumbled.

Garth smiled, pleased he had caught her off guard. "No need to panic, darling. I don't expect you to invite her into your home. She does, however, work with me. You'll undoubtedly be seeing her . . . and so will Craig," he added in an almost threatening tone. The smile faded suddenly when he said, "Jasamin is important to me, Deirdre. She isn't the same girl you met that day. All I ask is that you give her a chance."

Deirdre compressed her lips tightly to keep them from quivering. She told herself she didn't want to see Jasamin Grant again for Craig's sake, but that was only part of it. Jasamin may have been living and working with Garth in Central America for the past three years, but accepting that fact didn't make it any easier to see the girl with him now.

"I'll explain it to Craig," she said, refusing to acknowledge that her resentment stemmed from a jealousy she had thought was long buried. "Craig has never talked much about the accident, but I know it won't be easy seeing her again."

"I didn't expect it to be when I asked her to come," said Garth. "And in spite of what you think, it won't be easy for her, either."

Chapter Seven

"Who is she, Mommy?" Andy asked, clutching Deirdre's hand as they stood inside the terminal building.

Deirdre's eyes examined the woman in question. She had been attractive even after spending the night in the hospital, but that was nothing compared to the stunning creature that glided through the metal doors and directly into Garth's arms.

Their lips brushed and Deirdre felt a tightening in her stomach. It intensified when Garth reached down to take the case from her hand, encircling the girl's waist with his other arm.

"I already told you, Andy," Deirdre returned a bit testily. "Her name is Jasamin Grant. She's a special friend of your father's."

Jasamin wore a blue woolen suit to accommodate the suddenly cooler weather, and a silk shirt that was darker than her skirt and jacket. Over her arm she carried a white mink that complemented her fair beauty. A provocative slit ran up either side of the skirt, exposing an enticing expanse of thigh when she walked. On the whole, Jasamin's appearance made Deirdre all too conscious of the simple style of her purple shirtwaister.

Coming to the airport with Garth had been a mistake, Deirdre told herself. But curiosity had won out over common sense. She had even used Andy as an excuse, insisting he needed to get out of the house for a while, so as to avoid having to confess her curiosity. Now Deirdre wished she hadn't been so clever, or so curious.

Jasamin's head jerked suddenly when Garth spoke to her, and her eyes locked with Deirdre's. Finally, Garth brought Jasamin over and, to Deirdre's surprise, the girl extended her hand in greeting.

"Hello, Deirdre. It's nice to see you again."

"Yes," Deirdre said coolly, eliciting a frown from Garth. "This is my son, Andy. Say hello to Miss Grant, Andy."

Jasamin knelt to Andy's level and smiled. "Hi, Andy," she said. "You're as handsome as your dad, did you know that?"

Deirdre stiffened at this, but Garth was watching the exchange and didn't notice.

"Do I have to call you 'Miss Grant'?" Andy asked.

"I . . . well, no! If your mommy doesn't mind, you can call me 'Jassy,' like your dad. It's easier than Jasamin."

One side of his mouth lifted. "That's a silly name, Jasa . . . my."

She laughed and smiled up at Garth, then back to Andy, a gesture that annoyed Deirdre beyond reason. "It's Jasamin," she repeated for him. "My mother didn't speak English very well when I was born, but she liked the pretty yellow flowers growing outside her window because they reminded her of the color of my hair. So she asked the nurse what the flower was and the nurse told her jasmine, only my mother spelled it Jasamin. So, if it was hard for her, I imagine it would be pretty tough for a little guy like you. Let's just stick with Jassy."

"Jassy," Andy giggled. "That's silly, too."

"Well, you're a silly boy," she teased. "Let's go get my suitcases, okay, Andy?"

To Deirdre's surprise, Andy took her hand and they walked away together. So much for Andy's fear of strangers, thought Deirdre ruefully.

"Well?" asked Garth when they were out of earshot.

Deirdre shrugged indifferently. "Your flower has blossomed."

Garth laughed. "'A rose by any other name would smell as sweet,'" he quoted tauntingly.

"And a weed by any other name . . . is still a weed," she returned smartly, and moved off to the luggage carousel.

Once the luggage had been collected, they made their way through the busy terminal to the outside entrance.

"Why don't you two wait while I bring the car around," suggested Garth, setting the suitcases down on the sidewalk. Without giving anyone a chance to object, he scooped up Andy into his arms and said, "Come on, sport. You can go with me to get the car."

Andy rode quite happily in his father's arms, but after they were out of sight, Deirdre had nothing to concentrate on—except Jasamin Grant.

"How is Craig?" Jasamin asked, to Deirdre's surprise.

"Craig is fine."

Noting her brusque attitude, Jasamin drew a deep breath. "Why don't we talk about something else? Your son is adorable," she complimented smoothly.

"Yes, he is." Deirdre was little more than polite.

Jasamin moistened her lips. "Garth simply raved about him on the telephone. I don't think he expected Andy to be quite so . . . well, so receptive toward him. You could have made it difficult, Deirdre, but you didn't. Given the same circumstances, I don't think most women would have been so considerate."

Deirdre's brows drew together. "I love my son, Jasamin. Don't be so quick to judge a situation you know nothing about." The last thing she wanted was for Jasamin or Garth to misunderstand her reasons for giving Andy such a favorable image of his father.

Jasamin looked away uncomfortably. She appeared even more relieved than Deirdre was when Garth pulled up in front of them. He got out and put the cases in the trunk, then unlocked the doors for them.

"I want to ride in front with Mommy!" Andy demanded from the child's seat in the back. Deirdre had discarded the seat many months earlier, but insisted on using it again until Andy was fully well.

"You stay where you are, young man," Garth told him.

"I hate this dumb seat! I'm not a baby!" Andy cried.

"No one said you were," Garth returned. "You're in there because it's safe. Look, we'll all wear seat belts. Does that make you happy?"

"I'll sit in back with him, Garth," Deirdre said flatly.

"You'll ride with me where you belong," Garth barked with vehemence, his patience having run out completely.

Deirdre knew she'd made a mistake when Andy reiterated, "I want to sit with Mommy!" She had stupidly compounded his bad behavior just as she had in the hospital with the panda.

Nevertheless, her patience was wearing thin and she put in firmly, "I'm not up to listening to that for the next hour, Garth. Besides, I'm sure you and Jasamin have a lot to talk about."

"You wouldn't have to tolerate such behavior if you'd discipline the boy when he needs it," he argued sternly.

Jasamin shifted uncomfortably and Deirdre wondered if she wasn't reconsidering her earlier statement about Deirdre's kindness.

Not willing to tolerate such a reprimand in front of this girl, Deirdre snapped, "I didn't realize your experience with children was so vast, Garth."

Garth clenched his teeth. "Get in the car, Deirdre."

Deirdre knew he was right, but to admit as much in front of Jasamin Grant would have killed her. She got into the back seat beside Andy, who fell asleep before they even cleared the airport traffic. Because of this, Deirdre was forced to listen to the front-seat conversation. She soon learned that Garth and Jasamin spoke a language all their own, one that made her feel as if she had intruded on a very private meeting. They spoke in short, perfunctory sentences that they both clearly understood without elaboration.

It was an hour later when they finally reached the

house. Jasamin was staying at a hotel in town, and Garth drove her and Andy home first. If he was being considerate, Deirdre failed to realize it.

"I'll be right back, Jassy," said Garth, lifting Andy from the car seat without disturbing his sleep.

Feeling compelled to say something, Deirdre muttered a hasty good-bye before closing the car door behind her, and then climbed the steps after Garth.

"You don't give an inch, do you, Deirdre?" Garth asked. They had deposited Andy in bed for his afternoon nap and were standing outside Deirdre's door.

"I assume you're referring to the gardenia?" she jibed.

"Don't be flippant. It doesn't become you."

Deirdre stared at him icily. "What do you want from me, Garth? The last time I saw that girl she practically poisoned me with the venom from her pointed tongue. I won't even go into the things she said about Craig, who could have died for all she cared."

"She cared, Deirdre. If only you knew how much she cared." Garth pulled a hand through his hair. "I guess it's too soon to expect you to trust her, but for all our sakes, please try to see someone's side of this other than Craig's for once."

Deirdre turned to go into her room when she heard the loud crash from the living room below. She looked at Garth and raced down the stairs after him.

"Get out, you miserable bitch!" screeched Craig in anger. "You come near me again and I swear I'll kill you with my bare hands!"

Deirdre took in the scene with wide-eyed horror. Craig, who had spent the last two days in his room, was standing in the living room by the drink cart. From the way he staggered, Deirdre knew he'd been drinking heavily.

Her eyes moved to where Jasamin knelt on the floor. She was trembling as she picked up the remains of a crystal decanter. A whiskey stain marked the wall behind her. Deirdre knew Craig's aim had been low, but she could only attribute that to his drunken state.

"Dear God," swore Garth violently. "You slimy bastard!"

"No, Garth don't!" cried Jasamin, rising just in time to stop him from crossing to where Craig stood. "It's my fault," she sobbed. Tears had turned her mascara into dark streams on her cheeks. "I . . . I saw Craig at the window. I shouldn't have come in. I'm sorry . . . so sorry. Please forgive me."

Deirdre moved toward Craig. Why had she thought an explosion would do him a world of good?

"Craig, are you all right?" she asked with deep concern.

He drew his weak arm to his side and began to rub the pain away, just as she'd seen him do countless times. But this was worse. This time the pain went much deeper. "Make her go away." He sounded like a wounded child. "Can't stand anyone looking at me. Make her go . . ."

Deirdre felt as though she was caught up in some horrible nightmare—not her own, but Craig's. He had accepted the news of Jasamin's imminent arrival with surprising indifference, but now Deirdre could see that it had all been an act. What had Jasamin done to him before the accident that still caused him such pain?

Deirdre turned to find Jasamin enfolded in the shelter of Garth's comforting arms. For a moment Deirdre took a giant step back in time. "Jasamin and Craig won't always be between us," Garth had once told her. But if Deirdre had ever had the smallest glimmer of hope that those words were true, it was dashed in that instant.

Garth looked up then and his eyes met Deirdre's. There was an agonized look on his face, but Deirdre sensed it was because of what might have happened if Craig's aim had been better. It couldn't have anything to do with me, Deirdre thought numbly. He couldn't possibly be reading my thoughts. Suddenly Deirdre pulled her eyes away, and Garth silently led Jasamin from the house.

The evening meal Deirdre had prepared had gone cold.

She fed Andy earlier, and Craig had gone straight to his room without eating.

At ten o'clock Deirdre wrapped the slices of roast in foil and put them in the refrigerator.

She took a leisurely shower, all the while listening for Garth to return. In two days he hadn't been out of her sight, and in an odd sort of way, she'd gotten used to him. Their topics of conversation had been cautiously chosen, and were never of a personal nature, but Deirdre missed him all the same.

Deirdre went to bed in her own room. There had never been a question of her sleeping with Garth. For one thing, the master bedroom was too far from Andy's room. As far as Deirdre was concerned, that fact closed the issue, because she wasn't about to invite Garth to share her room.

By midnight Garth still hadn't returned, and shortly after that, having spent two restless and annoying hours, Deirdre finally slept.

Her dreams offered little comfort. That brief kiss at the airport . . . the smooth, comfortable conversation . . . the way Garth held Jasamin in his arms, stroking her long hair. The scenes meshed, conjuring up realities Deirdre didn't want to face. Realities she hadn't wanted to face ever since Roy had casually informed her that Jasamin was working with Garth. That had been almost three years ago, and Jasamin Grant was no longer a troublesome teenager. She was now a beautiful young woman, and obviously very much a part of Garth's life.

Deirdre woke from the lingering dream to the brightness of a cool autumn day. She lay in bed for some time, listening. For what, she didn't know. Some sign that Garth had come home, or that he hadn't. Home, thought Deirdre, rolling from her back to her stomach. She drew her pillow to her and hugged it tightly, forbidding the emptiness she had once known to invade her again.

Had Garth really come back because he felt threatened by Roy Carlysle? Deirdre couldn't imagine a man like

Garth ever feeling threatened by another man. Certainly not a man like Roy, whom she could never think of as anything closer than a friend.

Or could she? Deirdre wondered, bringing Roy's blond handsomeness to mind. She eased from the bed and walked toward the bathroom in a lethargic state. If Garth was willing to give her a divorce, given that Andy would be well taken care of, maybe she should start looking toward the future. Having a man in her life would certainly change things for her, but hard as she tried, she couldn't picture Roy as a candidate for that position.

Maddeningly, she could think of only Garth when the jet spray of the shower awakened the sensitive nerve endings in her body. A warm thrust of desire shot through her as her hands tenderly soaped the upturned swell of her breasts. The nipples were rock hard and longed for the moistness of his lips.

Damn you, Garth, Deirdre cried inwardly. It was beginning again. As each day passed, she had more and more difficulty denying the surrender her body ached for.

With a burst of anger, Deirdre turned off the hot water. She nearly cried out in horror when an icy spray of cold quenched the fire inside her.

The face of a stranger stared back at Deirdre as she sat before the mirror brushing life back into her hair. She hadn't seen that brightness in her green eyes for a long time. She had lost weight, but the prominence of her cheekbones was as attractive as the heightened color in her face. Her dark, thick lashes gave her eyes a mysterious quality that she didn't think even Garth Logan would be able to read.

The moment her thoughts turned to Garth again, Deirdre got up and walked away from the mirror. She shed her robe and stepped into her flesh-colored briefs and lacy bra.

She was standing at her closet, searching for her chocolate-brown dress, when Andy came bounding into her room. Knowing it was him, she didn't turn until she had drawn the dress from the closet.

"I thought we discussed knocking on Mommy's door before you come in, Andrew Logan." Only recently had Deirdre put a stop to his free access to her room. She didn't want to inhibit the child, but she had always felt a strong sense of privacy and recently Andy had become quite inquisitive.

"The door wasn't closed," Andy pointed out, rather smartly for one so young.

"He's right. It wasn't," Garth added, causing Deirdre to spin around wide-eyed, clutching the dress to her.

A lazy smile played about Garth's mouth and he took his time surveying her through hooded eyes. He stood leaning casually against the bathroom doorway, wearing what appeared to be nothing but a burgundy velour robe. His hair was tousled in a disordered but extremely sexy fashion. He looked like he had just gotten out of bed. Whose bed, she didn't care to guess.

"Daddy says we can go out for breakfast and then maybe we can drive down the coast to see the changing seasons. He worked reeee-al late last night just so he could spend the day with us."

Deirdre shot Garth a skeptical look he didn't miss. In fact, he stood away from the door abruptly and eyed her curiously.

"I'm afraid you and Daddy will have to go without me," Deirdre said, easing into her robe as casually as possible. "I've got to get back to work today, Andy. Poor Sally is probably exhausted by now, running the place by herself this past week. You know Debbie only works part time because of school, and . . ." She began to melt at the disappointed look on her son's face. "Another time, okay, Andy?"

"You always say that," he complained unreasonably, sliding off the bed and running past his father to slam the door of his room with a bang. Garth was right. Their son was a spoiled brat.

"When did you decide this?" Garth asked, walking into the room and closing the door securely behind him.

"Decide what?" Deirdre turned back to the dressing-table mirror and picked up a tube of lipstick.

"You know what, Deirdre. Why is work suddenly so important?"

Deirdre sighed. "I've been off since a week ago Friday. Andy is improving by leaps and bounds," she said, annoyed she should have to justify her decisions to him in the first place. "I can't let a child's whim dictate my schedule."

"Forgive me for thinking a drive down the coast might be good for us," he sneered. "You try coming up with ideas about how to keep Andy confined and still entertained. He's got at least another week before he's out of the woods."

"I know that, but Edith usually keeps him occupied with television or coloring books. I'm a working mother, Garth. That's all there is to it."

"You own the place, Deirdre," he reminded her sharply.

Deirdre threw the tube of lipstick on the dresser in a defiant gesture, one that made her look childish and stubborn.

"Deirdre's Boutique is not Saks Fifth Avenue, Garth. And in spite of what you think, it doesn't run itself. And"—she bit her tongue but the words came tumbling out anyway—"I can't work late at night just so I can be free for the day, as you seem to be able to do."

Garth tightened his jaw to control his temper. "Don't try it, Deirdre," he threatened.

"Try what?" She was smug, dangerously so.

"Don't try fabricating a relationship between Jasamin and me just to cover your affair with Roy Carlysle."

"You spent the night with her," Deirdre accused woodenly.

"We worked until three o'clock this morning," Garth said in defense. "The poor girl was ready to drop by the time we finished, especially after receiving Craig's abuse."

"The poor girl," Deirdre echoed cynically. "She's about as pitiable as a fire orchid in full bloom, and just as priceless."

The ambiguous remark left him cold. "My God, you're actually jealous of a schoolgirl!" He threw back his head and laughed suddenly. "Oh, God, Deirdre, you're driving me crazy."

"I'm glad you're amused." Deirdre carried her dress over to the bed and pulled it from the hanger in an angry movement. If I am jealous, she told herself, it's justifiable. He's living in my house and sleeping with her. What woman likes to be made a fool of like that?

"I don't like jealousy, Deirdre, but I'm glad to see it in you. It proves that the beautiful, excitingly sensuous woman I once knew is still very much alive. It's just a matter of pushing the right buttons to catch a glimpse of her."

Deirdre stood with her back to him, biting her lower lip. "I'm not a computer, Garth. And this isn't Dial-a-Feeling," she said dryly. "Now, if you don't mind, I'd like to get ready for work."

"But I do mind." His voice was low and husky, and he was so close behind her Deirdre felt his breath on her neck. Suddenly his hands were brushing her hair away so he could bend his lips to the creamy flesh of her neck and shoulder.

Aside from climbing over the bed, there was no easy escape from him. He was only testing, Deirdre told herself. If she didn't respond, he'd go away.

"I want you, Deirdre," Garth whispered, running his hands over her shoulders. She stiffened against him. "I've never stopped wanting you, and I don't think you ever stopped wanting me. If you had, Jasamin wouldn't trouble you so." Deirdre moved her shoulder when the tip of his tongue found the hollow behind her ear.

"I don't want to be late for work, Garth. Would you

please leave so I can get dressed?" Her voice sounded steady, but her pulse rate had doubled.

Garth's hands tightened momentarily, and then he slid his arms around her waist. "You came alive for me that night, Deirdre," he breathed huskily. "You were like liquid fire. I haven't forgotten and neither have you." His hand spread out over the flatness of her stomach, pressing her against him, deliberately making her aware of his male need. Deirdre pressed futilely against his arms but he refused to release her. "Stop this pretense, Deirdre," he urged. "Stop it before it's too late."

"I'm not pretending anything!" she cried, her breathless tone a betrayal in itself. "Garth, please, I don't want this!"

Swiftly, she was turned to face him and his mouth descended on hers. She struggled, but before long her rational resistance was washed away on a tide of emotion.

Deirdre was so lost in the velvety roughness of his tongue caressing the tender flesh of her lips, she didn't notice his hands releasing the silken sash of her robe until she felt his fingers brush her bare stomach.

Garth lifted his mouth a fraction of an inch from hers. "Touch me, Deirdre. Make it more than a dream," he urged. Only then did she realize her hands were clenched tightly, inches from his shoulders.

"No . . . Garth, please," she cried softly, feeling the invisible shield fall away.

With one hand Garth untied his own robe and pressed his nakedness to her. The clean scent of sandalwood reached her nostrils and Deirdre buried her face in his shoulder, drinking in the healthy scent she had long ago committed to memory. Taut fingers touched the damp hair on his chest, then relaxed as she began to trace a massaging pattern through it.

"Tell me, Deirdre. Admit you want me the way I want you." It was an urgent plea, born of an overwhelming need to hear the words.

Deirdre shook her head. Her body's betrayal was bad

enough. The words would turn a physical act into something more than she could handle. Having to admit her desire to herself was more than she could bear.

Garth pulled her to him more closely. "Then I'll make you admit it," he vowed.

His mouth covered hers again and the assault began anew. His tongue searched the warm hollow of her mouth, demanding that she respond in kind. Deirdre did so hungrily.

The bed was directly behind Deirdre, but it didn't prevent Garth from bending to draw an arm behind her knees and lift her into his arms. Deirdre hadn't the will or the strength to argue. He kissed her as he carried her to the side of the bed, and gracefully descended with her onto the mattress.

His hands were easing the robe from her shoulders when she stopped him. "Andy might come in," she said, surprised by the huskiness in her own voice.

Garth smiled softly. "I can fix that," he said, leaving the bed swiftly. Both doors were locked in seconds and Garth returned quickly to the bed as if he feared she'd change her mind. Indeed, those few seconds had given time for the doubts to resurface, but they vanished again as Garth boldly removed his robe and let it drop to the floor.

At a glance, Deirdre knew he was still the same powerful male animal she had been so physically drawn to four years before.

But this time it was very different, and Deirdre couldn't deny it. This time, if I let him make love to me, it will be because I want him physically. Nothing more. I don't love him, she thought. I can't. The cost of loving him is too high.

Garth was lying beside her again. His hands were warm against her skin as he released the front clasp of her bra with expert ease. Too expert, Deirdre told herself, tearing herself apart with conflicting emotions. She wanted Garth to make love to her, but her practical side warned her it would be a grave mistake. Garth was the same man, but she wasn't the same woman. Wanting him now was just a step away from loving him again, and she couldn't allow that to happen. She could be any woman in his bed. He didn't love her and he never had. She was the mother of his son, and he was there with her now because it was . . . convenient.

"What's wrong, baby?" Garth asked, sensing her withdrawal.

His thigh was bent across her legs and his arm attached itself firmly around her middle. "I can't, Garth. Please, just let me get up." Her words were shaky as her heart pounded wildly in her chest.

"I want you, Deirdre," Garth whispered urgently, his breath fanning her cheek. "Why can't you admit it's what you want, too?"

"Because I don't," she said, nearly choking on her tears.

Garth shifted his weight, but he was by no means ready to let her go. His hand moved back to cup her breast and his lips lowered to caress her nipple, as if to coax her into submission. His lips surrounded the rosy tip, and the velvety smoothness of his tongue sent a spasm of liquid heat through her.

"Don't, Garth . . . please," she whispered urgently, fearful that Andy would hear them.

Garth lifted his head again so he could look down at her. "Do you know what it's been like for me sleeping in that room down the hall?" he murmured softly. "It's all I can do to keep myself from coming in here each night after you've gone to sleep, just so I can sit and watch you when you don't have that guard up against me. I think about lying down beside you, Deirdre. I just want to hold you and know that you're real. You're my wife, Deirdre. I have a right to—"

"Don't tell me about rights!" she cried, closing her eyes tightly. "You wouldn't even be here if it wasn't for Andy."

A deathly silence fell between them. After a moment

Garth moved his leg from hers, but he lifted his hand to curve along her jawline. Deirdre opened her eyes to find him watching her intently.

"I won't bother to deny that, Deirdre, because I know it's too soon to make you believe anything else. You're so frozen up inside, it would take a blowtorch to thaw you out. But I'm going to, Deirdre. I'll find a way," he vowed, "I promise you that."

Deirdre drew a deep, shuddering breath in an effort to compose herself. "You seem to be very adept at understanding a woman's needs," she accused smartly. "Your experience must be vast indeed."

A tender smile touched his mouth and his eyes shone bright. "How can I make you realize you are the only woman whose needs I care to understand? I wonder, Deirdre," he said, stroking her jawline with his index finger, "if you fully understand your own needs. In fact, I'm beginning to wonder a great deal about you." He paused, trailing that same finger over her lips. "It's been a long time since you've let a *real* man make love to you, hasn't it, Deirdre?"

Oh, God, thought Deirdre, feeling as stripped emotionally as she was physically. Did he really expect her to admit she couldn't have born the touch of another man in all that time? She would never give him that satisfaction!

"You'd be surprised, Garth," she said brazenly.

Garth shrank away almost immediately, but not before Deirdre caught a momentary flash of pain in his eyes.

"Do you think I care how many men you've slept with since me?" Garth asked, rolling away from her completely. "If you're hoping to hurt me, you're wasting your time. And it won't stop me from wanting you, Deirdre. Maybe . . . just maybe I'm willing to share."

Deirdre would have stopped him then—if only to tell him that she'd lied about there being other men—but his words hit her so hard that she clung to the only defense she seemed to have left against him. Oh, she knew he had lashed out because she'd hurt him, but his words were too strong to be ignored. If he cared for her at all, he wouldn't be willing to share her with another man.

Garth stood with his back to her, pulling on his robe in short, angry movements.

"Why did you have to come back?" she asked weakly. "Why couldn't you have just stayed away and left me alone?" The thawing process he'd spoken of had already begun and Deirdre felt helpless to stop it.

If Garth was hurt by her words, he didn't show it. He didn't even turn to look at her.

"I had to come back, Deirdre. I had to find out for certain if you were real . . . or if you were part of a dream I once had." He walked toward the door leading to the hallway. With his hand poised to unlock it, he said quietly, "For whatever it's worth, Deirdre, that's a dream I've been carrying with me for a very long time. Even before I knew you had conceived my child."

Deirdre stared in wide-eyed disbelief. If he felt that way, why hadn't she heard from him in all that time? Why had he waited until now to come back? With those questions unanswered, Deirdre's doubts about him remained.

After Garth had gone, Deirdre dressed for work with a single purpose in mind. If Roy Carlysle had the answers, she was going to ask the questions.

Chapter Eight

Deirdre unlocked the glass door to her shop in the mini-mall that had opened the year she graduated from high school. At that time the store's owner was Lydia Brooks, a new woman in town who had left New York to recover from the loss of her husband in a car accident. She liked Deirdre on sight and hired her, despite her lack of previous experience. The salary wasn't anything to brag about, but Deirdre knew it was as much as Lydia could afford to pay summer help. Once Deirdre knew she could have the job on a permanent basis, she approached Lydia with a proposition. She would work for a smaller salary plus commission. The new store had yet to become a rousing success, as the mall wasn't completely rented out yet, and Lydia, seeing that it was to her advantage, agreed.

At first, only Lydia had benefited from their agreement. But Deirdre hadn't worried because she and Craig had still had plenty of her father's insurance money to live on and the house had long since been clear of debt.

Christmas was the turning point for them all. Lydia's mother became ill and Lydia had to return to New York. She hired part-time help so that Deirdre wouldn't be alone during the evening hours. During Lydia's absence Deirdre had rebuilt displays to fit her own youthful ideas. (Lydia was thirty-five and quite ancient in Deirdre's eyes.) As the Christmas shoppers began coming in to browse, Lydia's merchandise suddenly began to move, and Deirdre's commissions began to mount up.

She half feared being dismissed once Lydia returned,

but the cash-register receipts spoke for themselves. After the initial shock wore off, Deirdre suddenly found herself working side by side with rather than for the other woman. They planned eye-catching advertisements for the newspaper, and when the mall finally held its grand opening a year later, Lydia's Boutique held a fashion show right in front of the store. The place was never the same again.

Lydia had proved a good friend over the years, and now, as Deirdre walked around the empty store, she realized how very much she missed her. Her second marriage and return to New York had come at an opportune time for Deirdre as far as buying the shop was concerned. "It was always more your place than mine anyway," Lydia had teased during their tearful good-bye. They had written, but their letters had dwindled to only Christmas cards and birthday greetings.

Deirdre knew she had to make plans for Christmas now, even though the first frost wasn't on the ground yet. Somehow, though, she didn't want to think about that. What joy could this Christmas possibly bring, she wondered, giving in to a twinge of self-pity.

Deirdre was working diligently, trying to straighten out the books covering the past week, when Sally opened the store at nine. She came into the office with a fresh cup of coffee and a bright smile on her face.

"God, am I glad to see you here! Do you know I had three ladies who would not make a decision on a dress without getting your opinion first?"

Deirdre laughed pleasantly. "One of them didn't happen to be your mother by any chance?"

Sally giggled and tossed her dark brown curls. "Is it my fault my mother doesn't trust my judgment? Or that she obviously likes you better than she does me?"

Deirdre groaned. Any other time the running joke about Sally's impossible mother would have had her in stitches, but she had far too much on her mind now.

"Keep the customers at bay, will you, Sally? I've got a

million things on my mind today and if possible, I don't want to be disturbed."

"Does that include Roy?" she asked slyly.

Deirdre looked up at her. "Has he been in looking for me?"

Sally nodded. "He came by several times. I told him you'd probably be at home or at the hospital all week, but he . . . well, he seemed rather hesitant to call either place. I, uh, guess your husband being home might have something to do with it."

Deirdre frowned. "How did you know that?" Surely Roy hadn't taken to idle gossip!

"Oh, your housekeeper mentioned it." There was a gleam in Sally's eye. "It explained why Roy was so agitated all week."

Deirdre lowered her eyes to her work. "I see. Thanks for telling me, Sally. Why don't you put some music on. It just might bring in some customers."

Clearly that wasn't what Sally had hoped to hear. Naturally she was curious. But, although the girl wasn't malicious, she was not someone you confide your innermost secrets to.

"In other words, get lost, right?"

Deirdre laughed. "Right, Sally. Call me if you need me."

Debbie Baxter had a crazy schedule at school that allowed her to work two mornings and three afternoons a week, plus alternate Saturdays. Fortunately for Deirdre, Monday was one of the mornings she came in, so Sally didn't need her help on the floor. Deirdre would have time to catch up on the office work until both girls left for lunch. She certainly needed the time, because Sally had made a disaster of the previous week's records.

Shortly before noon, Sally knocked on the door and announced that Roy was there. Deirdre's feelings about seeing Roy were mixed, but after a moment's hesitation she told Sally to show him in.

Deirdre was standing with her back to the filing cabinets when Roy entered. His dark business suit enhanced his boyish attractiveness and when he smiled uneasily, Deirdre couldn't help but smile, too.

"How's Andy?" he asked, breaking the uncomfortable silence.

"Much better. I understand you went to see him at the hospital."

"Well, I thought . . . I mean . . . I hoped you'd be there. Not that I didn't want to see Andy, it's just that . . ."

"I understand, Roy. You didn't want to risk running into Garth."

His shoulders lifted and fell as he shoved his hands into his pants pockets. "He thinks we're . . . that you and I are . . ."

"Having an affair?" Deirdre supplied without censure. "Yes, I know. What I don't know is how he came to that conclusion."

"I never told him that, Deirdre!" Roy insisted, immediately on the defensive. "But I did let him know how I felt about the lousy way he's been treating you and Andy. And I told him it was possible you were becoming interested in . . . in someone else," he confessed.

Deirdre was torn between wanting to kill him and comfort him. She couldn't help but feel his separation from Olivia had something to do with his attraction to her, perhaps even that it had caused the separation. Until she knew for sure, dealing with this problem was virtually impossible.

"Did you tell Garth I wanted a divorce?" she asked boldly.

His head lifted. "No. Not like that. But if he got that message, then I'm glad," he declared adamantly.

"Roy, you had no right to interfere," she said, hoping to make him understand that there was simply no future for the two of them. He was like a young, vulnerable boy in so many ways.

Roy closed the space between them, but he made no attempt to touch her. "I can't stand watching what's happening to you, Deirdre. You've had to deal with so much alone. First Craig, and then Andy being ill so much, and even this place! It's all taking so much from you. You don't have any time left for yourself." He sighed wearily. "You need someone in your life, Deirdre. Garth doesn't even know you're alive. Darling, if it's the money, you know I would be happy to—"

"Roy, please! Don't say any more!" She cut him off abruptly, not wanting to listen to any more of his painfully accurate description of her life. Garth's absence had taught her that she was capable of surviving without a man in her life, but his return had made her realize that she wanted one there. But Roy Carlysle wasn't that man, nor could he ever be. If she needed proof of that, all she had to do was remember the way she had responded to Garth that morning.

Deirdre glanced at her watch. "I'm sorry, Roy, but it's time for the girls to go to lunch. I have to watch the floor."

Roy followed her out of the office and waited until Sally and Debbie left before broaching the subject again.

"Has it been difficult for you with Garth here?" he asked, keeping his voice low, so as not to be overheard by what few customers there were.

Deirdre shook her head but it had nothing to do with the way she felt. Of course it's been difficult, she wanted to say. He's making me come alive again and the thought terrifies me.

"He's been . . . very good for Andy," she said with a noncommittal air. "They've been spending a lot of time together. As a matter of fact," she said absently, turning her attention to straightening a rack of sweaters, "they were gone this morning before I even went down to breakfast."

Roy appeared shocked by her words. "Is Garth living with you?" he asked, loudly enough to cause one customer to glance their way.

Deirdre frowned at Roy. "You don't need to make it

sound so sordid, Roy. He wants time to be with his son. That's not so unreasonable, considering all Andy went through last week."

Roy moved closer to her. "Deirdre, don't you see what he's trying to do? He's using Andy to get to you!"

Deirdre glared at him. "Now you sound like Craig," she said critically. "Frankly, I wish you'd both stop interfering and let me make my own decisions about my marriage."

Roy was undaunted. "Does that mean you're considering ending it?"

Now Deirdre was surprised. "I haven't even thought about that. Not the way you mean."

"How many ways are there to end a marriage, Deirdre?"

She moistened her lips anxiously. "That's just not a decision I'm ready to make. Please, Roy, don't pressure me about this."

Roy extended a hand to rest lightly on her arm. "I won't, Deirdre. Not now. But I hope Garth's being here will make you realize how much better it would be if you allowed yourself to fall in love with someone else."

Roy didn't wait for her reaction. In fact, he seemed to shy away suddenly, and left, muttering something about calling her later.

It was almost seven o'clock when Deirdre let herself into the house that evening. She had stayed later than usual at the store and wasn't surprised to find the house quiet when she entered. What did surprise her was the light burning down at the boat dock; Craig must be working much later than usual, too.

Deirdre made her way to the kitchen and found Edith peering into the oven. "Edith!" she cried. "What are you doing here so late?" Ordinarily, once Andy was given his supper, Edith would leave Deirdre and Craig something on the stove and go home.

Edith looked up and smiled at her. "It was your husband's suggestion, and I must say it pleases me, too. He said he preferred to eat around eight and he thought, since you were working late, it would suit you better, too."

"Well, yes, but that makes a long day for you and it takes up your evenings."

Edith flipped her hand. "What's an old woman like me got to do anyway? Besides, Garth suggested I come in later in the mornings, since he's here to look after Andy. If I do, I'll let you know. It's going to be nice having a family around that dinner table again."

A family! Deirdre rolled her eyes, but didn't argue the point with her.

"Is Andy with his father?" she asked.

Edith shook her head. "He's with Craig down at the dock. He'll come home when he gets too cold. He's already had his dinner."

Deirdre didn't ask where Garth was; she didn't think she would like the answer she got. Instead she decided to take advantage of the facilities at the back of the house.

As part of Craig's therapy, a sauna and a hot tub had been installed, and Deirdre made full use of both. Craig generally used them every morning, but he also set them up so they'd be ready for Deirdre when she got home from work.

Deirdre found the whirlpool going strong, at 110 degrees. She pulled an oversized towel from the cupboard and fastened her hair up with a clasp.

She stepped out of her clothes and wrapped the thigh-length towel around her, tucking it securely between her breasts.

The eucalyptus steam hit her in the face the second she opened the door to the sauna, and she inhaled deeply. Every muscle in her body instantly relaxed as she stretched out on her stomach across the ceramic-tiled ledge.

After five minutes or so, Deirdre stepped out of the sauna and onto the octagonal wooden deck surrounding the hot tub of deep burgundy porcelain. She then shed her towel before stepping into the swirling water.

She laid her head back on the molded groove, submerging her shoulders in the water. The pulses of water tickled her feet as she stretched them out across the tub. She smiled to herself and moaned softly, feeling giddy and totally relaxed.

A trickle of water hit her nose, but when Deirdre pursed her lips to blow it away, she found her mouth covered by a firm yet undemanding one. Her eyes opened instantly and her hands lifted to push Garth's bare, warm shoulders away. But just as she realized he had come from the modified exercise room next door, she began slipping down into the tub. Now, instead of pushing him away, Deirdre grabbed at his shoulders as a gurgle of surprise escaped her lips.

"Come back here!" Garth ordered playfully, sliding his hands under her arms. Before she knew it, Deirdre was repositioned in the curved groove and Garth's hands were remaining in their highly suggestive positions near her breasts.

"Garth, let me go," she commanded stridently, much too aware of her own quickening pulse.

A menacing look finally forced him to do as she asked, but he did so with painstaking slowness.

His thick, dark lashes hooded his smoldering eyes as he watched her from his position on the wooden deck beside her. Deirdre could see he had on a pair of jeans that bore the telltale marks of physical exertion.

"I see you found the exercise room," she remarked, forcing her eyes away from his glistening torso. She knew if she looked for one single flaw in that athletic body, she wouldn't find one.

"Yes, I found it," Garth said, trailing his fingers through the water absently. "I hope you don't mind my using it."

Deirdre's eyes lifted, darting toward the closed door of the exercise room. She wondered briefly if that door had been closed when she first arrived, or if Garth had stood there unobserved watching her take her clothes off.

Deirdre looked away again, blaming the hot flush in her cheeks on the heat of the water. "No, I don't mind your using it. Why should I? You paid for it, after all."

"Did I?" he questioned curiously. "Oh, yes, I remember now. Roy is usually so thorough in his reports, it's hard to remember every little detail."

"How can you be so glib about all that money?" she asked, not wanting to discuss Roy.

Garth glanced around the room and shrugged. "I'd say it was well worth it. Particularly since it made the difference as far as Craig's ability to walk is concerned."

Her lashes fluttered. "You knew about that?"

"Yes, Deirdre, I followed Craig's progress very closely," he admitted with a sigh. "Believe me, darling, I wanted him to get well as much as you did." The endearment was so casual, Deirdre barely noticed it. She was more intent on the sweep of his gaze that took in the swell of her breasts and the water that swirled sensuously between and around them. Deirdre lowered herself further into the tub.

His fingers continued to trail in the water, moving suggestively close to her breast but not quite touching it.

"I wish you'd stop that," she said as though the action annoyed her.

Garth smiled softly and withdrew his hand from the water. "You're a contradiction, Deirdre. All cool and businesslike on the surface, but I suspect that underneath the surface there's a reserve of passion just aching to be tapped."

"You couldn't be more wrong," she returned saucily. But she was so disturbed by his words that she sat up and drew her knees to her chest protectively.

"I don't think so, Deirdre," Garth said, reaching out to tuck a wet tendril of hair behind her ear. His fingers trailed lightly over the pulse at her throat. "Only a woman capable of great passion would choose such an erotically stimulating way to relax after a hard day's work."

"I find it relaxing," she informed him defensively, and much too quickly to be taken seriously. In truth, she had never felt more alive than she did at that moment.

"Umm, perhaps," he acquiesced mildly. "You did look relaxed before I kissed you. I'm sorry I disturbed you."

Deirdre looked up then, expecting him to leave. When he didn't, she said smartly, "Don't feel you have to stay and keep me company." Her words completely contradicted her true desires. His presence may have made her a bit uncomfortable, because of her lack of clothes, but by no means was it unpleasant.

"Oh, but I do so enjoy your company," he replied with a knowing smile.

She would have gladly let him leave then, but he had no such intention. Indeed, when he stood he released the snap on his jeans and stepped out of them before she could react.

"Garth, what are you doing?" she cried, wide-eyed, as his thumbs eased under the band of his dark briefs, which stretched low across the flatness of his well-muscled abdomen.

"I think that's fairly obvious," he mused. "I'm going to join you."

He moved the briefs over his hips and Deirdre cried, "Garth, wait! I'll get out and leave the tub to you. If you'll just hand me that robe."

He laughed huskily. "Darling, the last thing I want you to do is run off. Besides, now that the crisis with Andy is over, you and I need to do some serious talking."

"This is hardly the place for serious talking," Deirdre argued as she glanced up at Garth. He was like a bronze sculpture, the sheen of his skin glistening as he moved toward her. He was as lean and muscular as she remembered him to be, yet he looked very different. Or perhaps it was she who was different. She wasn't seeing him through the eyes of a woman yet to experience the delights his body could bring. Now she was a woman who had known those pleasures, and denying his manhood was doubly difficult.

Garth stepped into the tub, reveling in her daring examination. To taunt her further, he lowered himself slowly into the water. Annoyed, Deirdre thrust a foot out when he least expected it, and Garth gasped as he plunged beneath the water.

When he didn't come up immediately, Deirdre's smugness turned to concern. But then she felt a hand grab her ankle and before she could catch the railing, she was under the water with him.

Deirdre's senses went wild as Garth's lips found hers in the hot, swirling depths. His flesh was like velvet against hers, and only her hands spread searchingly over the contour of his back reminded her of the hard, powerful strength of his muscles.

Garth's arms gently held her to him as he brought her to the surface of the water. She opened her mouth to breathe, as he had done, and instantly their tongues fired a passion between them. She touched him and tasted of him, letting her emotions carry her away more swiftly than the strongest of currents possibly could.

When his mouth finally left hers, he buried his face against her throat. "What was that you were saying about relaxing?" he asked huskily, tasting the beads of water on her skin with his tongue.

With her arms curled tightly around his neck, Deirdre reveled in the heady excitment his tongue was creating. I shouldn't be acting this way, she thought. I should be fighting him off, especially after the scene we had this morning. But she didn't fight. Instead she arched to him as the jets of water worked the column of her back. Oh, God, Deirdre thought, even the elements are against me.

"It is stimulating," she agreed, trailing her fingers through the wet thickness of his hair. "At least it is when you share it with somebody. I don't suppose you'd consider leaving, would you, Garth?" she asked halfheartedly.

Garth lifted his head and with a torturous groan, his

mouth came back to hers. "God, what you do to me," he muttered, taking short, nibbling kisses from her responsive lips.

They were on their knees facing each other in the center of the tub. The water no longer shielded her breasts from view, but that hardly mattered, as Garth sought what he was looking for with his hands. They molded the length of her rib cage, gently cupping the swell of each breast while his thumbs discovered the rosy tips and brought them to peak hardness with gentle caressess.

Suddenly, the kiss deepened as his hands moved to press against her lower back. Deirdre gasped against his mouth when she felt her hips drawn against his, making her aware of his desire.

"I need you so much, Deirdre," he whispered, moving his hands feverishly below the water along the provocative curve of her hips and thighs. "I can't be in the same room with you without wanting to touch you. I could make love to you right here, but it still wouldn't be enough. All of you has to belong to me, Deirdre. Just the way it did that night."

"No, Garth, don't. Don't!" she cried breathlessly, driven half wild by the patterns his fingers were tracing up and down her back, drawing her closer to him as he spoke. "It's not fair to keep reminding me of that night. It's not that way for me anymore."

His hands stopped at her waist. "It could be again if you'd just let it happen between us."

Deirdre shook her head, tightening her hands into fists at his shoulders. "I can't, Garth. You don't know what you're asking."

Garth pushed her away and positioned himself in the groove on the opposite side of the tub. He looked devilish with his dark hair pressed to his head, his eyes still smoldering from his slowly cooling passion.

"Is Roy that important to you, Deirdre?" he asked, taking her completely by surprise. She hadn't even been thinking of Roy. She was so caught up in her own desire, she could barely bring Roy's image to mind.

"Roy has nothing to do with this. Why do you keep insisting that he does?"

A sardonic smile curved his lips. "You saw him today, didn't you?"

Deirdre's eyes widened. "How did you know that?"

He shrugged indifferently. "That hardly matters. He obviously knows I'm living here now. Rather pompous of him to disapprove, if you don't mind my saying so."

Deirdre looked away suddenly. "Roy is merely concerned about me." Something you paid him well to be, she could have reminded him, but wisely didn't. That chapter of her life was closed as far as she was concerned. The only question now was her friendship with Roy; nothing beyond that mattered.

"I wonder if he would be half as concerned about a client he wasn't in love with," Garth sneered. "But you're not in love with him, are you, darling?"

Deirdre compressed her lips and remained mute. She was far too stubborn to respond to such a taunting question.

"If you were," Garth went on, "you wouldn't respond to me the way you do. I wonder if Roy realizes he's being short-changed in the romance department."

Deirdre sighed with frustration. "If you've come all this way just to break up what you *think* is going on between Roy and me, you've wasted a trip, Garth."

"Ummm, perhaps," he said, sliding down into a more relaxed position. "But then again, I may have timed this trip perfectly as far as our marriage is concerned."

Deirdre shot him a curious look. "What do you mean by that?"

He studied her face. "I should think that would be fairly obvious by now, Deirdre. I'm in love with you, and I intend to do whatever I have to to convince you to give our marriage a chance to work. Is that too much to ask?"

Chapter Nine

Deirdre smoothed some lotion into the tired lines around her eyes, then glossed her lips before dragging a brush through her freshly washed hair.

As she went through the motions of preparing for an enjoyable dinner, Andy sat perched on the water tank in the bathroom. He watched her as if thoroughly engrossed in every move she made, and giggled when she made a puckering sound with her lips.

"You haven't told me about your day, Andy," said Deirdre, adjusting the belt of her blue tunic. "Did you have fun on your drive with Daddy this morning?"

"We went to the museum where they have bunches of old, old, old boats. Then we went to meet Jassy and we took her out to lunch, and then all three of us went to Mr. Tanner's to see his boat. Daddy called it a sloop and Jassy said it was the most beautiful one she'd ever seen. We took it out for a sail and then we came home 'cause Daddy had some work to do."

Deirdre looked at him quizzically. "Your daddy sailed Mr. Tanner's sloop?" She was more than mildly impressed, knowing the magnificent vessel he was talking about.

Andy nodded proudly. "Daddy knows more about boats than anybody!" he bragged, causing Deirdre to smile.

She held out her arms to him. "Come on, tiger. Time for bed."

"That's what my daddy calls me all the time," giggled Andy.

Daddy, daddy, daddy, she thought as she carried the child into his room. She listened to his prayers, and, when he asked that his father be blessed, a chord struck in her heart. This time he spoke with genuine love, and it didn't fail to touch her.

After kissing him good night, Deirdre returned to her own room. Without Andy's small voice chattering, she was forced to consider a situation she wasn't certain how to deal with.

Garth had told her he loved her and asked her to give their marriage a chance. Whether she truly believed him or not was beside the point. The memory of how she responded to his lovemaking plagued her now. To deny that she wanted him would be futile. But to admit that she still cared for him was something else again.

What if I did let myself fall in love with him again, Deirdre wondered, glancing at her reflection in the mirror. She ran a finger lightly over her lips, still feeling the pressure of his kiss. What would we have to base a marriage on but a few days each year when our passion would be spent in each other's arms? Was it enough? Could she learn to live like that, waiting for his letters . . . waiting for him to come and see her and his son?

"No!" Deirdre exclaimed aloud, shaking her head to rid it of the thought. I could never do that! I'd much rather live without him completely.

He doesn't love me, Deirdre told herself, turning away from the mirror. Whatever he feels is physical, which is precisely what I feel for him. I learned a long time ago what results from a relationship based on sex, and I'm not about to let it happen again!

With that thought firmly in mind, Deirdre went downstairs to the kitchen to see if she might help Edith with the cooking. Edith shooed her out after giving her a peek at the succulent lamb she was roasting.

"You go and relax with the men," Edith urged. "I'll have it on the table in another ten minutes."

The thought of Craig and Garth together in the living room had Deirdre running to join them. Half expecting to break in on a fistfight, she was pleasantly surprised to find Craig sitting on the sofa and Garth standing before a lighted fire. They were talking about Craig's first and last love: boats.

"I didn't realize Tanner was looking to sell his sloop," said Craig with interest. "Are you thinking of buying it?"

"Thinking about it," Garth admitted. "I've been advised against buying a used boat, especially one as old as Tanner's. I've never seen a more attractive sloop, but appearances can be deceiving."

"That's for sure." Craig chuckled softly.

If Garth picked up on Craig's innuendo, he didn't let it show. Noticing Deirdre standing in the doorway, he smiled at her, then surprised her by saying to Craig, "I don't know all that much about boats. Do you think a guy like Tanner would mind if I brought someone along to check it over?"

Craig shrugged. "Why should he? He's asking a lot of money, so it must be in top shape."

Garth had poured Deirdre a glass of sherry and now brought it over to her. She smiled her thanks, but shifted a skeptical gaze between him and Craig. All she could do was wait to find out precisely what Garth was up to.

She didn't have long to wait.

"If you're not busy tomorrow, Craig, I'd like you to take a look at it with me."

Craig's head shot up instantly. "Me!" he exclaimed. "I didn't know you meant me!"

Garth turned back to face him. "I know you didn't. I wouldn't ask you if I didn't know what your opinion was worth," he stated boldly. "Fact is, you've built yourself quite a reputation around town. I'd appreciate your help."

Deirdre held her breath. She had never seen such a smooth delivery, but Craig was no fool. He knew when he was being manipulated and he recognized an expert at work.

Even so, Deirdre sensed he was interested in Garth's proposition. Garth couldn't have chosen a better way to get to him, she thought, and was touched by his effort to reach Craig.

Craig shot Deirdre a look, but she deliberately dropped her eyes so as not to influence him in any way. Finally, he said, "Why bother making that kind of investment if you don't plan on staying around here long?"

Deirdre didn't move a muscle, but she was acutely aware of Garth's hesitation before he spoke.

"If it's worth the money, I shouldn't have any trouble reselling it, if it comes to that."

"You mean if you decide not to stay long," Craig said pointedly.

There was a brief silence. "No," said Garth finally, sighing heavily. "I mean if I decide to buy it, then I shouldn't have any trouble selling it. Provided you're as much of an expert as people around here claim."

Deirdre felt a sudden tightening in her chest. Craig couldn't have made his question more clear, nor Garth his response more evasive.

"What time would you like to go?" Craig asked. Only then did Deirdre look up from her drink. Garth had been watching her, but suddenly he sounded anxious to end the conversation.

"Whenever you're free," he said, placing his glass on the cart. "Tomorrow, if it's convenient."

"Tomorrow afternoon, then," Craig agreed. "Ah, here's Edith, and I'm starved for a change. Ready, Dee?"

The dining room was used only on special occasions, which included the nights Roy dined with them. But even then, Deirdre had never known the table to look so lovely. It was set with English china, her mother's favorite crystal, candles glowing at either end of the table, and a low arrangement of autumn flowers in the center; one couldn't help but be impressed.

"You should feel honored, Garth." Craig grinned from one side of his mouth. "Roy gets the everyday china."

Deirdre resented this sort of maliciousness from Craig, particularly when Garth didn't deserve it. But Garth was undaunted by the tactless remark. As he held Deirdre's chair for her he said, "It's always nice to feel welcomed in a strange home. Even if it is by the housekeeper."

Deirdre smiled inwardly, wishing she knew how to handle Craig as smoothly as Garth did.

If it was Edith's intention to impress Garth with her culinary skills, she didn't miss her mark. They were feasted with cups of oyster stew followed by crisp salad greens in a tangy vinegar-and-oil dressing. The lamb was served in perfect slices with mint jelly and asparagus, and there were baked apples for dessert. Brandy was served along with coffee in the living room afterward.

Although Craig reveled in the meal, Deirdre suspected that Garth had forced himself to do it justice as much as she had. He was subdued throughout, leaving her and Craig to make polite small talk. It struck Deirdre then that she and Craig hadn't really talked in a very long time.

Craig finished his brandy and rose abruptly. "If Edith is ready, I think I'll walk her home. I could do with some fresh air."

After they had gone, the silence stretched between Garth and Deirdre until she rose to leave.

"I'm rather tired, so I think I'll turn in. Good night, Garth."

"Won't you have another brandy with me?" Garth asked, taking a step toward her.

Spreading her hands over her skirt front, Deirdre shook her head. "I don't think I could stand another. I'm a bit light-headed as it is."

"We could take a walk," Garth suggested. "The moon is full and the crisp night air would clear your head."

"No, I don't think so. Maybe another night."

"Deirdre." His voice stopped her at the door. "Will you

at least think about what I said? Is it too much to ask after all this time for us to try to make a go of our marriage?"

With her back to him, Deirdre closed her eyes to the pain his soft, caressing voice was inflicting. "You wanted some time with your son. That's all I can give you, Garth. Please don't ask for more."

"Deirdre!" he called, but she was already halfway to her room. She ran the rest of the way, praying he wouldn't come after her and try to force her to admit what she knew in her heart. She would have gladly given their marriage a chance to work, but not if she had to settle for his being gone most of the time living in some nightmarish country filled with violence and danger. And she wouldn't ask him to give that up, having made that promise to him long ago. It was his world, his life, and as much as she needed him, she would never ask.

In the three days that followed, Deirdre saw little of Garth. He spent his days with Andy, and, although he joined her and Craig for dinner each night, he made no attempt to seek out her company afterward. Instead he would closet himself in the study and work late into the night.

On Thursday, Deirdre left the store in the early afternoon in order to take Andy for his postoperative checkup. Andy couldn't wait to get home and tell his father the good news. His enthusiasm forced Deirdre to face what had been on her mind for days. For Andy's sake, as much as her own, she had to find out precisely what Garth's plans were. If he was leaving soon, she wanted to prepare Andy.

The minute they walked into the house, Andy made a direct line for the study, where he knew his father would be. Deirdre followed him in but stopped short when she saw Jasamin sitting behind the desk pounding on a typewriter with the aid of earphones, while Garth stood behind her proofreading some other papers.

"Jassy! Daddy! Guess what! I get to go out on the boat with you every day now that I'm all well! The doctor said!"

Garth scooped him up in his arms and hugged him tightly. "Now, that is good news, isn't it, Jassy?"

Jasamin's eyes moved unsteadily from Deirdre to Andy and finally to Garth. "It is good news," she said with a half smile. "I, uh, think I'll take some of this work back to the hotel with me and finish there."

Garth was genuinely perplexed. "But that's crazy! You're almost finished and . . ." He paused, catching sight of Deirdre standing stiffly in the doorway. "Oh, I see," he said smartly. His eyes locked with Deirdre's, his expression suddenly grim. "That won't be necessary, Jasamin. We'll leave you alone, so take all the time you need."

He didn't speak again until he had closed the door behind himself and Deirdre. "Edith is baking some cookies for you, Andy," he said, placing his son back on the floor. "Why don't you see if they're ready."

Andy didn't need to be asked twice. "Let's take a walk, Deirdre," Garth suggested after Andy had raced away. Stopping only long enough to collect his windbreaker, he ushered her outside.

Deirdre looked out toward the boat dock. She made out Craig's form as he walked along the deck of the newest vessel docked there. The Tanner sloop put the others to shame. For all the attention Craig gave to it, one would have thought it was his own.

"Before you explode," Garth said, "I think you should know Craig is fully aware that Jasamin has been coming here to work each day. In fact, it was his suggestion."

Deirdre looked at him doubtfully. "A suggestion you cleverly maneuvered him into making no doubt. I'm surprised Craig allowed himself to be taken in so easily."

"There was nothing easy about it, but don't give me all the credit," he sneered. His hands slid into the pockets of his blue windbreaker and he led the way in the direction of the dock.

"I suppose the credit should go to daffodil in there," Deirdre mused caustically.

"On the contrary. I had to practically force her to come and face him again. Granted, they keep their distance, but at least there's a civility between them now that undoubtedly would never have existed if you'd been around making sure Craig had his crutch."

"Just what do you mean?" She stopped dead, the color drained from her face.

"Just what I said, Deirdre. As long as you're there for him to lean on, he'll never stand on his own. Why should he? It's much easier to let Mommy do everything for him. Don't tell me you have never drawn comparisons between Craig and Andy."

"Craig is not a child!" she said defensively. "Nor is he some mental case."

"The hell he isn't!" Garth argued with vehemence. "When you're not there, he drinks just like he did the day Jasamin arrived. He didn't have you around to console him—to remind him of all the horrors he's had to suffer because of her."

"He has suffered," Deirdre cried in anguish, clenching her hands at her sides. "You don't know about the months he lay helpless in that hospital bed. Or the pain he went through thinking he might never walk again, or the greater physical pain he felt every time he tried to walk and failed."

"But he did walk, didn't he, Deirdre? In spite of the fact that you were there to pick him up, he managed to pick himself up occasionally. For God's sake, Deirdre! Let him fall! Let him bruise his pride right along with his knees." His eyes bore pleadingly into hers. "And for Craig's sake, let him come to terms with Jasamin in his own way, in his own time. If you love him at all, let him do this one thing by himself."

Deirdre was so hurt by his words, she struck out blindly. "I want that girl out of my house!" she cried hoarsely. "And I don't want to ever see her here again."

She started away but Garth hauled her back so roughly she stumbled against him.

"Let go of me!" she cried. "You have no right!"

"I'll let you go as soon as you answer one question. Do you want Jasamin to leave because of Craig, or is it because you think she and I have something going?"

A stab of pain shot through her heart and she struggled futilely to be free of his hold. Garth shook her soundly.

"Say it, Deirdre! Damn it, if you believe it, then say it!"

Her hands bit into his forearms. "Why should I, when you'll only deny it?"

"I deserve that chance at least."

"Like hell!" she flung at him. "I owe you nothing, Garth. Just get out of my life once and for all!"

"No!" He gasped in a throaty whisper. There was a perceptible change in the way he was holding her. "Deirdre, no. I love you. Doesn't that mean anything to you? Don't ask me to set you free."

Tears were streaming down her face, blinding her. She hadn't known he was going to kiss her until the salt taste was pressed to her lips. Deirdre felt an explosion inside then, as though a dam had burst, releasing a wealth of pent-up emotions. She wrenched her mouth from his and brought her hand to the side of his face. The sound seemed to crack, and was followed immediately by an electrified silence.

Deirdre stared in horror and brought the offending hand to her mouth to still its quivering.

"I didn't mean to do that," she said in a barely audible whisper. "Garth . . . I'm sorry."

He didn't seem to hear her. He turned away and strode back to the house.

Deirdre remained where she was for several minutes. As hard as it was to admit, Garth had been right. Not wanting Jasamin there, in truth, had very little to do with

Craig. Jasamin was an extremely beautiful young woman who, for the past three years, had worked closely with Garth. Deirdre resented that almost as much as she resented the obvious affection Garth and Jasamin shared. She was jealous, pure and simple.

The sting of the cool breeze from the bay made her cheeks smart. Deirdre rubbed them with the back of her still stinging hand. She hated herself for having slapped Garth, and vowed to keep a tighter rein on her emotions in the future.

Rather than return to the house, where she was bound to see Jasamin and Garth, Deirdre made her way to the dock. Upon arriving, she saw Craig jump onto the wooden planks from the deck of the boat with more agility than he had displayed in years.

"Hey, what are you doing down here?" he asked. "This is supposed to be a surprise for you." His eyes darted to where *The Deirdre* was painted in beautiful script along the side of the boat.

At first Deirdre didn't know what to think. A fantastic thrill shot through her. If Garth had planned on reselling the boat, he certainly wouldn't have gone to the trouble of . . .

No. That wasn't necessarily true. The boat could always be repainted, or perhaps he intended giving it to her as a gift. Was that why he had been so evasive the night Craig questioned him about it? No wonder he wasn't worried about reselling it. Perhaps he thought that when he left, this grand and expensive gift would make up the loss for her and Andy.

"When was this done?" Deirdre asked, her heart slowly resuming its normal beat.

"Couple of days ago," Craig told her, a brightness shining in his eyes that Deirdre noticed instantly. He was happy. Truly happy. "She's a beauty, isn't she? In my opinion they haven't built anything in years that can compare. Want to go below?" he asked encouragingly. "She's been redesigned from stem to stern. Garth spared no expense."

Deirdre shoved her hands into her pockets. "I . . . no, I don't think so, Craig. Some other time," she said, resisting the urge to take him up on his suggestion. It didn't seem right, somehow.

Craig's head jerked and then he smiled. "I get it. You want to wait for Garth to give you the grand tour. Well, I guess it's his right."

"Yes, I guess it is," Deirdre agreed softly, wondering now if Garth would ever want to be bothered with her again. "You really enjoy this, don't you, Craig?"

He looked at her curiously. "Working on *The Deirdre*? Sure. Why not?"

She shrugged. "No reason. I was just curious. You had just seemed so resentful of Garth, and I . . ."

Her words died as she watched the crease deepen between Craig's brows. The light faded slowly from his eyes and Deirdre could have kicked herself.

"Garth is paying me to do this," he said dryly. "I told him he didn't have to, since he covered all my medical expenses, but he said that didn't matter. Who am I to argue?" he said rather smartly. "Money is money, after all."

Suddenly Deirdre felt a heaviness in the air between them. She wished she could say something to make it right again, but words failed her. She was his crutch, Garth had told her. "*He drinks when he doesn't have you around to console him—to remind him of all the horrors he's had to suffer.*"

"Will you sail the sloop when it's finished?" Deirdre asked on a lighter note.

"I doubt it," he told her flatly. He bent to sort through the tool box, but when Deirdre turned to leave, he said, "Is Jasamin still at the house?"

Deirdre moistened her lips. "Yes, at least she was when I left. I think . . . she was about to leave," Deirdre admitted guiltily. Drawing a deep breath, she asked, "Does her being here bother you, Craig?"

"Andy needs to be home, where he can rest properly," he said, "and Garth is intent on spending as much time with him as possible. It seemed the most logical solution."

"Then it really was your idea," she said, feeling even more foolish for attacking Garth as she had.

Craig sighed as if bored by the subject. "We stay out of each other's way," he admitted dryly. "Besides, she'll be gone soon, anyway."

Deirdre's heart skipped a beat. "Did she tell you that?"

Craig's eyes were on her suddenly, causing her to shift uncomfortably. "Garth said she was flying to New York tomorrow to spend a few days with her family, now that their work is nearly finished. I don't know what their plans are after that."

The phrase "their plans" cut through Deirdre like a knife. She wished she could be indifferent to Garth's leaving, but it wasn't as simple as she thought. Particularly not if he was leaving with Jasamin Grant.

"If you don't mind, Deirdre, I'm overhauling the auxiliary motor and I'll need all the daylight I can get," Craig snapped testily.

Duly dismissed, Deirdre returned to the house. Garth's car was gone, which meant he and Jasamin were gone as well. She should have been glad, but instead a feeling of intense guilt assailed her. If Garth was right, she was doing Craig a terrible disservice by thinking him too weak to deal with his feelings for the girl.

Deirdre's hopes of speaking with Garth again that evening were dashed. When dinner was served, there were two places set, and Edith offered no explanation concerning Garth. Naturally, she would assume his wife would already know, and Deirdre couldn't bring herself to admit that she didn't.

The meal was difficult to get through. Craig's enthusiasm had dimmed without Garth there to keep it fanned, as Deirdre now realized he had done continually.

"Craig, we should go someplace tonight," she said with forced cheeriness. "We haven't been to a movie in a long time. We could see if Edith would mind staying with Andy, and we could see what's playing in town."

Craig looked at her as if he thought she'd gone mad. "Are you asking me out on a date?" he teased laughingly.

Deirdre smiled. "Why not? We used to go out together all the time. Remember how we used to play tennis, and go skating, and even swimming!" she cried enthusiastically. "That indoor pool is open at night, and we could . . ."

The lines that creased his face made Deirdre acutely aware of her thoughtlessness. Craig could do all those things if he wanted to, but she knew how conscious he was of the scars he bore. Her emphasis on swimming had turned him off completely.

Craig began to shake his head. "I'm really bushed tonight, Dee. But if you want to go out someplace, I'll keep an eye on Andy for you."

Deirdre bit her lip. "Craig, please. You never get away from this house anymore." Garth's words were drumming in her head, but she plunged ahead recklessly. "Darling, no one cares if you can't—"

He pushed away from the table abruptly. "That's the crux of it, isn't it, Deirdre? No one cares! No one gives a damn!"

"I care, Craig!" Deirdre was on her feet instantly, reaching out to him. "Craig, I love you. You know I care—"

"I don't want your love!" he screeched violently, thrusting an angry fist into the air. "You're smothering me with it, Deirdre! You always have and I can't stand it anymore! I'm not some wind-up toy for your amusement. I can't smile when everything inside me is hurting, and I can't pretend the way you do that tomorrow is going to be better . . . and brighter . . . and perfect! It doesn't get better for me, Deirdre. The pain lessens but it's always there inside me, eating away a little bit more each day. It doesn't go away!"

After he'd gone, Deirdre sat in silence, trying to cope with the overwhelming sense of despair that enveloped her. She felt a gentle hand on her shoulder and looked through a film of tears at Edith's concerned face.

"He didn't mean it," she soothed. "You're all he's got and he's just afraid to love you too much." She pulled out the chair to Deirdre's right and sat facing her. "It was like that for me when I lost my husband. I had all those children to take care of by myself. After several years I found a man I could truly care about again, but rather than risk going through the pain of losing again, I decided I'd rather be alone." Her hand covered Deirdre's. "Craig has lost so many times in his young life. First his folks and then yours. And in a way, he lost that girl Jasamin." She paused with understanding. "I think you know what I'm talking about, Deirdre. It isn't really so different for you. I've watched you with Garth, and I know—"

"It's not the same thing," Deirdre cut her off sharply. Edith meant well, but this time, she'd hit too close to the truth. "I'm sorry, Edith. I don't mean to take it out on you."

"I know, child. Maybe I take too much on myself sometimes." She paused. "What you need is a good night's sleep. Go on up and I'll bring you a nice cup of tea with honey."

Deirdre shook her head, knowing she couldn't face being alone in that empty room wondering if Garth was with Jasamin.

"I think I'll take Craig up on his suggestion and go out for a while. Maybe I'll see a movie."

Edith smiled. "I think that's a good idea. If it's all right with you, I'll just spend the night and look after Andy if his daddy doesn't come home early." The silent admission being that neither was sure Craig would be in any condition to look after himself, much less the child.

"Thanks, Edith. You're such a good friend."

It seemed fated that as Deirdre passed the telephone in the hallway, Roy should call. Roy had always been there for her and, although she knew she was being selfish, she asked, "Care to join me at a movie tonight?"

There was a short silence. "What? I mean, yes! Of course! I was just calling about those papers you dropped off at my office, but I guess Lady Luck is with me for a change. I'll pick you up in ten minutes. All right?"

"Sure, ten minutes will be fine. Oh, and thanks, Roy. I really need a friend tonight."

Deirdre changed quickly into a dress with small, colorful flowers on a black background. The Oriental collar and cap sleeves made for a tight-fitting bodice that accented the firm roundness of her breasts and the slimness of her waist. The skirt was straight, with a slit up either side, giving Deirdre a much sexier look than she had intended or was even aware of.

Deirdre donned a long-sleeved black jacket of the same material as soon as Roy arrived. He refused a drink, leaving Deirdre to suspect he feared running into Garth. Come to think of it, though, Deirdre preferred not to see Garth as well. She was relieved by the time Roy's silver-toned Mercedes was speeding off into the night.

"You look beautiful, Deirdre," Roy said, shooting her a glance across the darkened car interior. "I was afraid after our conversation the other day, you wouldn't want to see me again."

Deirdre smiled fondly at him. "I value your friendship too much to ever let that happen," she confessed.

Satisfied, Roy launched immediately into a conversation concerning a movie he wanted to see, and Deirdre agreed indifferently.

"We've already missed the early show and it doesn't run again until ten-fifteen. Let's go have a drink first."

Deirdre agreed with a nod and made a firm resolve to enjoy herself that evening. Perhaps a drink was just what she needed.

She had hoped for a quiet lounge somewhere close, but Roy parked the car in the lot of one of his favorite haunts. The flashing sign that read LIVE ENTERTAINMENT was the last thing she wanted to see.

"Couldn't we go somewhere else?" she asked.

Roy laughed, reading her expression. "It's not as bad as you think. It's a Country Western band but there are two separate lounges. One's for dancing, but the other is more intimate."

Deirdre didn't like the sound of that, but allowed him to guide her inside all the same. The room where the band played was packed and the other was a haven for secret lovers.

She was about to object when Roy glanced at his watch and said, "We'll just have time for one drink before we have to leave for the show. Not too loud for you, is it?"

After a moment's hesitation she shook her head and followed him to the table.

"Bacardi cocktail, darling?" Roy asked, slipping into the mood of the room.

But Deirdre barely noticed the endearment. "What? Oh, yes, that sounds fine." She was distracted by the attractions of the room. It was separated from the other lounge by a glass divider, through which one could view the dance floor and the band. The partition absorbed the excess noise, and only pleasant strains of music reached their ears. "This really is quite nice," she remarked after Roy had given the waitress their order.

"I thought you'd like it. Now, aren't you sorry you never let me bring you here before?" he asked, leaning slightly toward her.

Deirdre smiled. "I'll reserve judgment until I taste my drink. I never thought a bar would be high on an attorney's list of preferred places to discuss business."

"Well, that's just it," he said, daringly trailing a finger along the pulse at her wrist. She withdrew her hand from the table, and Roy sighed heavily. "I was hoping that, for just one evening, business wouldn't be our main topic of conversation. You know, you can destroy a man's masculinity by only talking about business."

Deirdre arched a brow. "I dare say you've found other consolations," she teased with a familiarity that disturbed her. Even jokingly, she and Roy had never talked this way before.

But Roy merely shrugged. "Men do, you know. But they tend to remain emotionally detached from sex. That is, until they find a woman they truly love, and then . . . well, let's just say he's putty in her hands."

Deirdre moistened her lips. "You must have felt that way about Olivia once," she said, but she wasn't thinking of Roy and his estranged wife. Garth said he loved her, but four years was a very long time. If Roy's theory was true, Garth could have had dozens of other women, and would probably continue to have them even if she did agree to what he had asked. "How do you suddenly lose that emotional bond when you've truly loved a person?"

"Maybe you never really do," Roy said softly. "The love dies, certainly, but sexually . . . maybe you never really forget what it was like being with that one person. I guess the key is to find someone who's better for you in every way, including bed. Then you start building new memories and the old ones just lie dormant."

Yes, thought Deirdre, that's the way it had to be. If she couldn't forget Garth, she should find someone better.

Deirdre was thoughtfully silent until their drinks came. Once they did arrive, Deirdre was feeling the effects after only a few sips. Her emotional exhaustion and the potent drink combined to make her want to seek oblivion.

"Go easy, sweetheart," Roy urged gently. "I wouldn't want to have to carry you home, even though the prospect of having you in my arms is very tempting."

The atmosphere had also mellowed Roy. Deirdre extended a hand to cover his. "Thank you, Roy. For being the best friend I could ever have."

The muscle of his jaw twitched, but then he smiled and covered her hand with his free one. "Why don't we dance, before we start getting maudlin here."

Deirdre glided willingly into his arms once they reached the dance floor. They moved quietly to the rhythm of the music for some minutes before it changed to a faster-paced song.

"I don't think I'm up to this," Deirdre admitted. She took his hand as they made their way through the crowd back to their table.

"We should leave soon," Deirdre said, leaning close to be heard over the suddenly loud music of the fast-paced song.

"We have time for another drink if you—"

The words caught in his throat as his eyes registered surprise. Deirdre followed his gaze to a nearby table that sat in a darkened corner. Deirdre couldn't mistake the flash of blond hair, but she wasn't concerned with Jasamin Grant at the moment. Her eyes locked and held with Garth's as he sat casually in his chair. By the state of their drinks, Deirdre could tell they had been there awhile. Deirdre's hopes that Garth had just noticed them as well were dashed when he leaned forward and brought his face into the light. Clearly his anger had been smoldering for some time.

"I guess we'd better say something," Roy suggested. But even as he spoke, Garth and Jasamin were rising. Garth threw some bills onto the table and led Jasamin from the bar without so much as a backward glance.

"I'm sorry, Deirdre," Roy muttered softly.

"It's not your fault. He's been angry with me all afternoon."

"That wasn't anger in his eyes," Roy informed her. "I wish to God it had been," he said in a strange tone. "Come on, I'll take you home."

"No," Deirdre said abruptly. "I don't want to go just yet. Besides, if he's out with Jasamin, I certainly don't have to feel guilty for being here with you."

Roy sat back with his hands folded before him. "As much as I'd like to give Garth enough rope to hang himself, I can't do it, Deirdre. Not where that girl is concerned."

"I don't understand."

He sighed and rubbed a hand briskly over his face. "I should have told you the truth about her a long time ago. Especially after she went to join Garth in his work, but I . . . well, I didn't think you'd care to hear her name, much less what happened to her."

Deirdre swallowed convulsively. "What did happen to her?"

"Jasamin had a serious breakdown, Deirdre. I didn't hear about it until a few days after the accident. When Garth spoke to me about looking after you, he also mentioned that he was afraid of what was happening to Jasamin. She was hysterical one minute, subdued the next. Finally, she just fell apart completely."

Deirdre felt numb. "Are you saying . . . she had a breakdown because of the accident?"

Roy nodded. "She couldn't bring herself to face Craig, but she assumed full responsibility for it. She spent a year in the hospital. When she was released, she was an entirely different person. She was mature, responsible, gentle, and probably more vulnerable than she'd ever been in her life."

"And that's when she went to be with Garth."

"Yes. Garth sent for her, even though she was of legal age."

"He must care very much for her," Deirdre said weakly.

Roy shrugged. "I guess, in a way, he's always felt responsible for her. She couldn't have been more than ten or eleven when Garth married Jennifer, but she was a younger version of her in every way. Rich, beautiful, and spoiled."

"I didn't realize you knew Garth then. He never told me about his ex-wife," she admitted.

"There wasn't much to tell. He married a spoiled heiress and she married an ideal. They made a fabulous-looking couple but Jennifer wanted the society life of New York and Paris, and Garth's work took him to Central America. They weren't married more than a few months before Jennifer divorced Garth and married some big-shot architect."

"What happened to Jasamin then?" she asked. "You said Garth always felt responsible for the girl."

"Well, yes, but Jasamin spent a lot of time in European boarding schools until her father's death a few years later. There was a big blow-up between Jennifer and Garth when Jasamin's custody and control of her inheritance went to him. Garth snatched her out of school abroad and enrolled her here in the States. Jennifer didn't mind that, except she thought the school should have been in New York." Roy made a face that showed his disapproval of Garth's ex-wife.

"The problem was," he continued, "Jasamin and Jennifer were very close at the time and Jasamin rebelled against Garth's authority. When Jasamin had her breakdown, Garth stuck by her, but Jennifer . . . well, she virtually turned her back on the girl. I suppose they've worked that out now, but, at the time, if Garth hadn't sent for her, she would have had no one . . . and no place to go. I honestly don't think she would have made it on her own."

Deirdre lowered her eyes. "No wonder Garth is so . . . protective toward her."

"Yes, he certainly is that, but that's all he feels for the girl, Deirdre. I shouldn't have let you believe otherwise. When Garth told me Jasamin was coming here, I urged him to tell Craig about her breakdown, but he wouldn't. He said that was something the two of them had to work out for themselves. I guess he was right, judging by the way you've reacted to the information."

Deirdre's thoughts swept back to the time when all this must have taken place. She remembered Roy telling her that Garth's life wasn't as uncomplicated as it seemed. Had he been referring to Jasamin's breakdown? That would certainly explain why Garth had so readily agreed to the proxy marriage.

Deirdre shook her head to rid herself of the thought.

Would knowing about Jasamin and her reason for joining Garth really have made a difference? The circumstances of her marriage would still be the same. If Garth loved her as he claimed to, he would have made some attempt to see his son. But there was nothing, not a word.

"Deirdre, please don't be upset about this," Roy urged, dragging her thoughts back to the present. She looked at him in confusion and realized that she must, indeed, look upset. "I would have told you about Jasamin's breakdown, but at the time I thought it best not to. I didn't think it would have helped the situation any."

"No, no, it wouldn't have helped." Not where Garth and I are concerned, she added silently. "If I'm upset, Roy, it's because I realize how unfair I've been to Jasamin. Garth tried telling me before I ever laid eyes on the girl how . . . well, how fragile and insecure she was. I'm afraid I wasn't easy to convince." She drew a hand over her forehead. "I hope I can make it up to her somehow."

Chapter Ten

Deirdre was still thinking about Jasamin Grant when she let herself into the house sometime later. She climbed the stairs to her room, but upon reaching the door, she stood motionless and stared down the hallway to the master bedroom. A light burned beneath the door, but Deirdre acknowledged Garth's presence with mixed feelings.

As tired as she was, Deirdre didn't think she could sleep unless she spoke to him about what she had learned. Maybe if she could make him believe she was genuinely sorry for her hostility toward his ward, he would at least meet her halfway.

Deirdre kicked off her shoes so as not to wake Craig or Andy. She walked the length of the hall and tapped lightly on one of the double doors. There was no answer, and with much bravado, Deirdre pushed down on the handle and went in.

She stopped dead when she realized the room was empty. Perhaps he's downstairs, she thought, but then she heard the door close behind her. She turned to find Garth, clothed in only his bathrobe and locking the door behind him.

"I want to talk to you, Garth." She spoke with a nervous quiver in her voice that she couldn't seem to control.

"Isn't it nice we had the same idea." He smiled, but the smile didn't reach his eyes. "I was waiting in your room for you," he explained when she looked at him curiously.

"You wanted to talk to me?"

His laugh was short. "Not exactly. Perhaps I overstated

that a bit. But it hardly matters, since the goal is achieved. We are indeed in the same bedroom, just as all husbands and wives should be in the middle of the night."

Deirdre's chin lifted a fraction of an inch. "You're angry with me about Roy," she stated flatly.

"How very perceptive of you."

Deirdre drew a deep breath. "We were going to go to a movie, but after we saw you, we just went for a drive," she admitted, hoping to satisfy his angry mood without developing one herself. The last thing she wanted was to argue with him again. Such misery had to be taken in small doses.

"It's rather late for a drive, isn't it?"

She swallowed hard. "Roy and I had a lot to talk about. I didn't realize how late it was getting."

"Do you really expect me to believe that you and Roy talked until three o'clock in the morning?"

Deirdre stiffened when he moved closer to her. "If you're implying what I think you are, I've already told you Roy and I are not involved." The upward tilt of his mouth angered her beyond reason. "This is ridiculous, Garth. We don't have a conventional marriage and I don't have to answer to you every time I decide to have a drink with a friend. Besides, you've already told me that you don't care."

"I care, Deirdre," he said huskily. "You'd better believe I care. Whatever is going on between you and Roy stops now!" he seethed vehemently. "You're my wife, and I don't share my wife with any man."

His hands reached out and slipped beneath her jacket, and Deirdre made no attempt to stop him from sliding it off her shoulders. He was just angry enough to tear it off, if it came to that, and although she didn't give a damn for the jacket, she didn't want to add fuel to Garth's anger.

"Roy and I are not having an affair, Garth!" she said emphatically. "Why can't you believe that?"

Garth didn't seem to hear her as he worked the buttons of her dress. More slowly now, he slid the garment off her body, fitting his hands along the curves of her hips and thighs in a kneading fashion that caused her to breathe unsteadily.

"Garth, you said you wouldn't force . . ." She got no further as his hand came back up to release her bra. It was gone in seconds and her breasts fell free of the confining material.

"I won't use any force," he said as his hands tested the firmness of her breasts before lowering his mouth to taste their sweetness. "I know you as well as I know myself. Surely you haven't forgotten."

If she hoped to defy his arrogance, she was quickly losing the will to do so. As Garth eased away her half slip, along with the remainder of her undergarments, Deirdre found herself wriggling free of the silken fabric instead of fighting him. She felt the tip of his tongue make a circular pattern around her navel, and when he pressed his lips to the sensitive area, her fingers bit into his shoulders.

"You're not going to stop me this time, are you, Deirdre." It was a statement, not a question.

Deirdre waited until he was standing again before she spoke. "No," she said quietly. "I'm not going to stop you."

His eyes searched hers. "Why?" he asked. "I need to hear you say it."

Deirdre swallowed against a tightness in her throat. She would have looked away, but Garth moved his hand to hold the side of her throat with light force.

"Why, Deirdre?"

"Because I want you," she said, her tone thick and sultry.

The smile was gone from his face when he bent his head to hers. His mouth played across hers, coaxing her lips to part with playful sweeps of his tongue.

Deirdre moved her hands inside his velour robe and moved it easily off his shoulders. Her arms strayed around his neck and she pressed the length of her body to him. From the moment her fingers met the curl of hair at the nape of his neck she was carried back in time, and the memory of that night came flooding back in vivid detail.

Garth's hand reached out to switch off the lights, and the room was cast in total darkness. Then, suddenly, his arms came around her waist and lifted her. Garth carried her to the bed, his mouth never leaving hers, and laid her back on the downy softness while lowering himself effortlessly beside her.

Garth rolled onto his back, carrying her with him. He held her close, raining kisses across her face and throat, while her thick veil of hair covered them. When he pushed her hair back, he circled the inner curve of her ear with the tip of his tongue, sending spasms of delight pulsating through her. No man could know her the way he did, she thought. How eagerly she submitted to the physical needs of her body when Garth touched her, arousing her as only he could! He knew instinctively the secret places of her body that brought her the most pleasure, and he explored each at his leisure.

This preliminary lovemaking was blissful torture, and Garth reveled in his power over Deirdre to the fullest. Just when she thought she couldn't stand any more, he changed positions with her and his body surged yet more passionately against hers.

Reality floated dimly somewhere outside of Deirdre. She heard Garth's whispered words like the rumbling of a gathering storm when he said, "Tell me the truth, Deirdre. Is Roy the man you want making love to you now?"

Deirdre quaked, knowing he had done this deliberately. He was using the ultimate weapon to make her admit she wanted him, and not Roy. He had taken a gamble, she thought, but it would have paid off. But why had he risked the fulfillment they could have had if he had said nothing?

"No," she said simply, but there was a wealth of anguish in her tone.

"Oh, God," Garth moaned in agony, aware of the hurt

he had caused. But they both knew there was no turning back. Their union was made complete, spiraling to a pinnacle they both sought, but it had nothing to do with love, and that fact alone made the descent almost unbearable.

Deirdre woke alone to the pale light of dawn. Her eyes searched the dimness of the room for Garth, but he was gone. Then she heard it, and the sound stirred her. In the far distance, the air sang with the unmistakable honking of the Canadian geese as they made their way to the tidewaters of the Chesapeake.

Deirdre retrieved Garth's robe from the end of the bed. He seemed to have laid it there for her, but somehow this morning she couldn't imagine him being that considerate. Tying the robe about her, she went to the window just in time to watch the sky fill with the fabulous birds. Every year was the same, but Deirdre never tired of the sight. Soon, hundreds of thousands of the winged creatures would dominate the bay shores, along with the whistling swans and ducks.

Craig invariably slept through the arrival of the northern fowl, so when Deirdre spotted the *Jessy Bess* out in the cove, she knew Garth had been unable to resist the call of the birds.

Or had it been the thought of waking up alongside her that had driven him out so early?

Unwillingly, the memory of their lovemaking came to clear consciousness. Deirdre felt an overwhelming sense of shame for having allowed it to continue after he had asked the question he'd been saving for just that moment. But to turn back at that point would have been impossible. She should never have let it happen in the first place. The seeking of pleasure from the use of each other's body could in no way be called *making love*.

The aftermath had been bittersweet. There was nothing they could say to each other to make it right. Their selfishness had tarnished what they had once shared.

"Mommy! Mommy! Look outside!" Andy burst into

the room like a shot. In his excitement, he didn't even pause to wonder why his mother wasn't in her own room. He raced to the window and she scooped him into her arms and carried him out onto the balcony in spite of the crisp autumn morning.

Deirdre remembered sharing the sight with her father for years on end. She knew exactly how Andy felt, only just now being old enough to appreciate it. She was so glad to share it with him.

"Oh, Andy, it's so wonderful here," Deirdre cooed softly, holding his shivering body close to her own. "If I didn't have you and this magnificent place . . ." She said no more.

Andy tipped his head back. "Where's Daddy? Why are you wearing his robe?"

Deirdre compressed her lips. "Daddy is out there on the *Jessy Bess*. See the sail?"

"But he promised to take me sailing!" Andy insisted petulantly. "He wasn't s'posed to go without me!"

"You were sleeping, Andy. Next time, okay?"

Andy squirmed out of her arms and returned to the warmth of the room, passing a jeans-clad Craig on the way.

Craig looked uneasily at Deirdre, then smiled. "Thought you'd be up with the geese. Don't those miserable birds know some people like to sleep in?"

Deirdre managed a laugh as she turned away. "Guess not. You usually manage to sleep through it."

"Yeah, with a pillow over my head."

Conversation was strained between them, as Deirdre had expected it to be. But she wasn't going to be the one to make it right, not this time; this was something very different, and they both knew it.

Suddenly Craig's arms came around her waist and he pressed a kiss onto her hair. "Forgive me, Deirdre. I've been a fool."

Her hands trailed over the hair on his forearms and she dropped her head against his chest. "It's not your fault,

Craig. You didn't tell me anything Jasamin Grant hadn't already told me a long time ago. Even Garth tried, but I . . . well, I didn't want to listen."

"Yes, well, we Mallorys are good at not wanting to listen," he mused. Craig released her and walked over to stand by the balcony railing and stare out over the water. His eyes fell on the lone sail. "I did a lot of thinking last night, Dee. Ordinarily I'd take a bottle of scotch to bed with me so I don't have to think, but last night . . . we were out of scotch," he said with a forced laugh, making light of a very serious situation.

"Craig, if you don't want to talk about this—"

"I think it's time I did, don't you?" he cut in firmly, flexing his shoulder muscles tautly. "It's easy to blame other people for your mistakes, and that's what I've been doing all these years. That accident was *my* fault, not Jasamin's . . . and not Garth's." He turned to face her then and she could see how much that single admission had cost him. "I used to tell myself that if it weren't for Garth, the accident would never have happened. I didn't even know Jasamin had a guardian until that day. When she told me how strict he was, I knew he wasn't going to sit idly by while his seventeen-year-old charge went off on a weekend fling with some guy."

Deirdre shifted uncomfortably. "You weren't wrong about that," she said dryly.

"Yes, well, as you can see, I wasn't in any frame of mind to be grateful when Garth paid the medical bills, or . . . well, when everything else happened," he added shyly.

Deirdre's chin lifted. "You mean when he married me to give his child a name."

Craig nodded. "Look, Deirdre, I know how hard it's been on you with Garth coming back here, and I haven't exactly made it any easier. I just want you to know that whatever you decide, I'm behind you all the way."

Craig had clearly drawn some conclusions from her state of dress, but Deirdre said nothing to alter his opinion. It was enough to know he was finally coming to terms with his own feelings for Garth. In time, Deirdre knew she would have to do the same.

She was driving to work when she recalled the things Roy had told her about Jasamin Grant. She also recalled Craig saying that Jasamin was leaving for New York today. If she were going to see her, it would have to be now.

Deirdre drove to the Bayview Hotel, where Jasamin was staying and where Garth had stayed the week Andy was in the hospital. But once she arrived, she was hesitant about going in. She intended to begin by discussing what she'd learned with Garth, since she didn't know how receptive Jasamin would be to seeing her. But her determination finally overcame her doubts, and a few minutes later, Deirdre was knocking on the door of Jasamin's room.

Jasamin was dressed in casual slacks and a blue-striped linen shirt with the tail hanging out. She greeted Deirdre with wide eyes, but it was only a moment before Jasamin was composed enough to speak.

"We must be on the same wavelength. I was going to come by the store later, to see you. Please come in, Deirdre."

Deirdre stepped into a typical hotel room, which was nothing like the expensive suite she had expected to find. Somehow the words "rich and spoiled" no longer applied to Jasamin.

"I hope you don't mind my coming by without calling first," Deirdre said, noting the suitcases lying open on the bed. "Craig told me you were leaving today, and I didn't want to miss seeing you."

Jasamin turned and strode slowly across the room to where her suitcases lay. "You know about my breakdown, don't you?" she asked directly.

After a brief hesitation Deirdre nodded. "Roy told me last night. I'm very sorry, Jasamin. I'm afraid I wasn't very kind to you after the accident."

A smile touched Jasamin's lips. "Why should you have been? As I recall, I sounded like a hysterical, malicious bitch. If anyone should be apologizing, it's me."

Deirdre licked her lips, then walked over to where Jasamin stood. "Craig told me this morning that he blames no one but himself for what happened. It's taken him a long time to admit that, Jasamin, but now that he finally has, I'd like to think it's just a matter of time before we can all put it behind us once and for all."

Jasamin clutched the dress she was folding. "Craig is being very cavalier, but the accident wasn't his fault. Not entirely, at any rate. Oh, he was driving, but he was very angry . . . very upset by the things I'd said."

"What did you say?" Deirdre prompted.

Jasamin drew a deep breath. "I told him I was in love with someone else, and I was only using him to make . . . the other man jealous."

"You mean Garth, don't you." It was a flat statement.

After a pause Jasamin nodded. "I can't remember a time when Garth wasn't the center of my life. All those years I was away at school, he wrote to me more than anyone else. He sent me pictures and presents, even after he and my Aunt Jennifer were divorced. I was so sure that when Garth became my guardian, he would come and take me to live with him." She gave a small laugh. "It didn't quite work out that way, so I started rebelling against him. I tried everything imaginable to make him angry, but it didn't work."

"Until Craig," Deirdre said knowingly.

"Until Craig," she agreed softly. "Two months before the accident, I started telling Garth about Craig in my letters. Oh, I was always very careful not to mention his name, but the things I did tell him would have made your hair curl," she confessed, wincing at the pain of the memory. "I didn't even give a thought to Craig's feelings. I met him through a girl I roomed with, who was dating his best friend," she explained. "But Garth didn't seem to believe me about Craig until . . . well, until we went away together that weekend."

"The weekend of the accident," Deirdre affirmed, beginning to see why Jasamin felt so guilty and Craig so victimized. "Craig never told me about that weekend."

"I was sure he hadn't when I saw him again. That kind of hate doesn't last four years unless it's bottled up inside."

"Or unless someone you love very much has hurt you terribly." Deirdre knew then that Craig hadn't been completely honest with her about why he resented Garth so much. Perhaps he hadn't even realized it himself, but she was confident that he would.

"By the time I realized Craig felt the way he did about me, I was in well over my head. I explained about Garth being my guardian, but that seemed to make things worse. For what it's worth, Deirdre, Garth has never given me the slightest encouragement." Deirdre began to wonder if her thoughts weren't written across her face. But Jasamin continued, unperturbed. "After I went to work for Garth, I realized I didn't stand a chance with him. Even though he never talked about you, I knew he thought a lot about you and Andy."

"This really doesn't have anything to do with Craig," Deirdre said tactfully, not wanting to discuss Garth with Jasamin.

"I know, Deirdre, but I think it's important for you to know how Garth and I feel about each other now." Deirdre stiffened noticeably, but Jasamin continued unburdening what was on her mind. "We're very close, Deirdre. As close as friends can possibly be." She paused briefly. "As far as Craig is concerned, I would do *anything* within my power to make up for the hurt I've caused him."

Deirdre smiled, feeling strangely relieved at having heard Jasamin admit that she no longer loved Garth. It was as if a heavy burden had been lifted from her heart.

"If you're willing, Jasamin, I think I can give you the

chance to work things out with Craig. But you would have to postpone your trip for a few days."

Jasamin didn't hesitate to smile in agreement.

More than once that day, Deirdre questioned the wisdom of her actions. Inviting Jasamin to stay at the house could prove to be a big mistake if Craig's change of heart proved to be only a momentary mood.

Deirdre also realized that Craig might still have tender feelings for Jasamin. If he did, he could end up even more hurt than he was already. Deirdre sighed with self-disgust. Here she was again, trying to second-guess Craig's feelings and trying to protect him from getting hurt. When would she ever learn that Craig was a grown man, not a boy any longer? He could take care of himself, and that meant dealing with his feelings for Jasamin Grant on his own.

One other thought was in her mind as she drove home that evening. With Craig no longer a major concern in her life, Deirdre knew she would be forced to deal with her feelings for Garth. All she knew for certain was that their marriage could not continue as it was. Either she had to make a commitment to him on his terms—which meant accepting the fact that he would be away from her for all but a few weeks each year—or she would have to make a complete break from him. That thought alone left her on the brink of tears.

Deirdre forced a smile when she entered the house a few minutes later and heard music and soft laughter coming from the living room. She stared wide-eyed at the familiar faces of several weekenders who used their boat dock. They had been to the house before, but Deirdre couldn't remember a time when they were there all together.

Craig stepped away from the group and came toward her with a smile. "Guess what? We're having a party." He grinned. Deirdre thought he looked younger than he had in years.

"No kidding! When did this happen?" Deirdre smiled at Lisa Templeton, a woman she knew and liked well. Lisa was an artist and Deirdre had sold several of her pen-and-ink sketches of the bay in the boutique. Orders for more had allowed the woman to quit her librarian position and concentrate on her talent full time.

"Oh, you know what it's like," said Craig. "Everybody keeps saying what a great idea it would be, but nobody ever does it. So I made a few phone calls, and *voilà!*"

Deirdre smiled her approval. Craig was like a different person and, although she knew he had taken only a small step, at least he was moving in the right direction. Deirdre couldn't be happier. Edith had once said Craig was crippled not in his body, but in his mind. Happily, he was on the road to a complete recovery.

"I'm glad you're in the partying mood, Mr. Mallory, but have you considered how we're going to feed all these hungry people?"

He spread his hands. "No problem. The beer and wine are on ice, and Garth and some of the guys are out back starting the crab boil. As host, I felt it was my duty to stay and entertain the women."

"Ah, I thought as much," she teased. "Well, don't let me detain you a moment longer. I'll just change my clothes and make myself useful elsewhere."

Craig laughed. "Don't forget our houseguest. She's working her tail off in the kitchen shucking oysters, and turning quite green the last time I looked. I'm afraid the girl will never make a true Marylander."

Oh, poor Jasamin, thought Deirdre, hurrying to change into jeans and a sweater before heading back downstairs to the kitchen. Jasamin was indeed quite ill from the sight of the oysters, and Edith had asked her to make the cocktail sauce instead while she worked up batches of spoonbread.

"I'll never get the hang of this, Edith," Jasamin complained mildly, shifting her hair back with her shoulder. "I never was very good in the kitchen."

"You'll learn, dearie. You'll learn." Edith beamed and gave a sly wink to Deirdre.

"Has anybody seen Andy?" Deirdre asked.

"Out with his dad," Edith informed her. "He's been fed and he's ready for bed but I don't think you'll budge him without a fight."

Deirdre started out but a word from Edith stopped her. "Here, take that one with you before she passes out on me." She jerked her head in Jasamin's direction and chuckled softly.

Jasamin was clearly delighted to be freed from her task, and didn't wait for a second bidding. "I'll shower and change and be down in a sec," she called before scooting out.

Outside, Deirdre found Andy playing with the only other child in the group. The seven-year-old girl had him literally jumping through hoops for her.

Deirdre smiled at this, then lifted her eyes from Andy to his father, whose eyes bore gently into hers. She hadn't seen him since the night before. The day's activities had mellowed her feelings about their lovemaking, but the strain it had caused lay heavily between them. Deirdre longed to throw herself into his arms, knowing his desperation had stemmed from his fears about Roy. She understood, because until that morning, she had secretly feared Jasamin in that same way. But Deirdre couldn't let her defenses down so easily. Not until she was certain that she was ready to commit herself to him on his terms.

Or let him go completely . . .

Her thoughts were interrupted abruptly when she heard Andy cry, "I can, too, sail my daddy's boat anytime I want!" Deirdre turned to find him facing little Karen with his hands planted firmly on his hips, daring her to defy him.

"Oh, Andy, you're just a baby. Babies don't know how to do anything," she added, all-knowing.

"Don't call me that! I'll show you—"

"That's enough, Andy," Garth cut in sharply, reaching

them at the same time Deirdre did. "If you don't behave yourself, you won't be able to join the party. Now run and play, both of you, and no more bickering."

The children ran off, leaving Garth and Deirdre to face each other alone. He looked comfortable in his light blue velour shirt with the sleeves pushed back over his forearms. His dark jeans fit snugly over his lean, well-muscled hips and thighs. Deirdre responded instinctively to his attractiveness with a sharp intake of breath. It would always be this way, she thought. Other attractive men would come and go throughout her life, but she would never respond to any other man as she did to Garth. He was the only one for her, but he would never be totally hers.

"It's much cooler than I thought," Deirdre said, trying to excuse her sudden trembling.

"Strange," he said with a smile, "I was just thinking how warm it was getting." He moved a step closer to her. "Jasamin told me you'd invited her to stay for a few days. Thank you for that, Deirdre. It means more to me than I can say."

Her lashes lowered. The last thing she wanted from him was gratitude.

"You convinced me to let Craig come to terms with Jasamin in his own way. I just hope I did the right thing."

"I'm sure you did," he said with a reassuring smile. Suddenly he took Deirdre's hand in his own, warming her cold fingers against his palm. "Look, Deirdre, I know this isn't the time or the place, but I want you to know how sorry I am for . . ."

His words died and the hand that held hers contracted tightly around her fingers. He fixed his eyes behind her as he said grimly, "Well, there he is, and right on time, it seems."

Deirdre turned to find Roy watching them, standing off to the side. "What do you mean, right on time?" she asked. But before Garth could respond, they were interrupted by Lisa Templeton.

"Deirdre, how nice to see you again. It's been ages since we've had a chance to talk."

"Yes, Lisa, it has been. Have you met my husband? Garth, this is—"

"Oh, we've already gotten acquainted," Lisa cut in. "Actually Garth and I have mutual acquaintances in Washington. I guess I don't have to tell you your husband moves in some pretty important political circles."

"No, I didn't . . ." Deirdre bit back the words, hating to admit that this woman knew more about her husband's work than she did.

"Lisa's exaggerating," Garth said wryly. "But even if you weren't," he said, directing his words to Lisa, "I wouldn't bore Deirdre with the details of my work. We have far more important things to talk about."

"Well, yes, of course you do. You see each other so seldom, one wonders that you'd bother talking at all."

Deirdre's cheeks colored and she was extremely grateful for the cover of darkness. Two years ago, when Lisa first started coming to the bay, she was newly divorced. She was attractive and excruciatingly shy, with very little confidence in herself or her talent as an artist. But that was the old Lisa. The new one could make suggestive remarks without batting an eye.

Typically, Garth took such a remark in his stride. "I promised you a tour of the boat, Lisa. Since my wife has other guests to see to, I suggest we take it now."

Deirdre didn't miss the barb, but she was far too conscious of Garth's casualness with this stranger to be affected by his words. In a huff, she turned and walked over to Roy, who stood with a can of beer in his hand.

"Hi, Roy. What are you doing here?"

"What do you mean, what am I doing here? I was invited!" He sounded put out by her gruffness. "Didn't he tell you?"

Deirdre was aghast to hear that Garth had invited Roy after what had happened the night before. "No, he didn't tell me. Why would he invite you without telling me?"

Roy shrugged. "I wasn't sure you were working today, so I called here to tell you I had those quarterly tax reports ready for your signature. He suggested I bring them out tonight, since there was going to be a party."

"How cozy," she sneered. What could Garth possibly have been thinking of, to invite Roy here? Was he satisfied that Roy was no longer a threat to him? But if that was true, why did he sound so annoyed when Roy arrived?

"Deirdre, you're not angry with me, are you?"

Sighing wearily, Deirdre shook her head. "No, of course not. I just think it's rather strange that Garth would accuse you of having an affair with me one minute, and then invite you to a party the next."

"Deirdre! I didn't mean—"

"Mommy! Mommy! Mommy!" Andy's heartrending cry reached them just before he threw his small arms around Deirdre's legs. Tears were streaming down his face and he sobbed convulsively when she bent to pick him up.

"Andy, darling, what is it?"

"D-D-Daddy sp-spanked m-me!" Andy was crying so hard, his breath coming in choking gasps, that Deirdre feared he would pass out.

Before she could calm him down enough to find out what had happened, Garth had reached them and took Andy from her arms.

"Garth, don't! He's frightened!" she cried.

"He'll be more than frightened if I ever catch him untying the boat from the dock again. A second later, Deirdre, and he would have been trying to sail the damn thing."

Deirdre's heart pounded with fear at the thought of what could have happened to Andy, and she followed Garth as he carried the child into the house.

Andy kicked and screamed until Garth finally dumped him unceremoniously onto his bed. "Get into your pajamas, Andy, and then into bed." His voice was controlled, but just barely.

"You promised to take me sailing!" Andy dared to say, obviously never having confronted a grown-up's temper before. Craig had simply ignored such tantrums and Deirdre was ashamed to admit she had catered to them.

"You don't deserve to go sailing. You don't get rewards when you behave badly, Andy." He unbuttoned Andy's shirt and stripped it off. "Until you can promise me you'll never do something like that again, you won't be allowed near the boat dock. If you go there without permission, you will be spanked again."

Andy was still too hurt to understand why Garth had punished him so severely. He pulled away from his father, blubbering until he looked quite ill.

"I hate you, Daddy," he sobbed. "I wish you'd go away and never come back."

When Andy announced that he was going to be sick, only seconds before he began to retch violently, Garth paled. From past experience, Deirdre knew Andy had to finish before she could take him into the bathroom to clean him up.

Garth trembled visibly. "My God, I didn't realize . . ." His words were barely audible to Deirdre who had picked Andy up and carried him into the bathroom. Garth followed and stood silently in the doorway, looking as hurt as his son had only a few minutes earlier.

Deirdre stripped the rest of Andy's clothes away as the tub filled with water. "He'll be all right, Garth. Go back to the party. I'll put him to bed and join you later."

By the time Deirdre had changed the bed, Andy was still sniffling, but he had calmed enough for her to tuck him in, kiss his cheek, and leave him for the night.

"I love you, Andy," she whispered sweetly across his cheek.

"Does Daddy still love me?" he asked innocently.

"Yes, of course he does. Daddies don't stop loving their

little boys just because they do something they're not supposed to."

Andy looked bright-eyed. "He won't . . . go away, will he?"

Deirdre's heart wrenched with pain and she realized the moment of truth had come. Lifting a hand, she pushed his hair off his forehead.

"Sometimes, Andy, daddies have jobs that take them far away from their families. They can't help it. That's just the way it is. Your daddy has a job like that and it's . . . well, it's very important to him."

Andy comprehended her words as much as a three-year-old could. But he still looked puzzled. Then, with a weary sigh, he turned on his side and closed his eyes.

"I'm going to ask Daddy if he'll stay here and live with us," he announced with a loud yawn. "I think he'd like that."

Deirdre didn't have the heart or the strength to try and make him understand why he couldn't ask that of his father. But she didn't worry about it, either. Knowing Andy's short memory, she doubted he'd mention it again.

After he dropped off to sleep, Deirdre returned to the party. Craig and Jasamin came toward her immediately. "Everything all right, Dee?" Craig asked. He and Jasamin had been talking quietly together, but Deirdre was too exhausted to give their apparent pleasure in each other's company more than a passing thought.

"Oh, yes, Andy's fine now. Learned his lesson, I hope," she added, her eyes lifting heavenward.

"Garth's heartsick over this, Deirdre," said Jasamin. "Maybe if you talk to him?"

Deirdre spied Garth then. He was standing with Roy beside a tall oak tree. Clearly, he was still troubled, but not because of his son. Garth looked ready to punch Roy in the face.

"Yes, I'll speak with him later." She drew a breath, knowing what a coward she was being. If there was an explosion between the two men, she wasn't about to get caught in the middle of it. "That crab boil smells delicious. What's in it?"

Craig, too, had noticed Garth and Roy, and he seemed inordinately pleased by the sight of them. One would have thought he'd staged the scene himself.

"Suddenly I'm hungry, too. What about you, Jasamin? Care to sample the feast?" he asked.

Oblivious of what was going on, Jasamin shrugged and said, "Lead the way!"

Chapter Eleven

For the next hour or so, Deirdre mingled with the guests, gliding easily from one topic to the next, as though all this socializing were old hat to her. Part of this she attributed to the wine she had had with her meal, but she realized for the most part she was just making a concerted effort to avoid being alone with Roy. Since his private conversation with Garth, Roy had appeared unusually anxious about something and Deirdre didn't doubt for a moment that it had something to do with her. But, whatever it was, Deirdre was in no mood to discuss it tonight.

Deirdre had been thoroughly attentive to the discussion about new movies going on between the Gleasons and Tom Rossi until she happened to glance up and find Garth standing on the far side of the dying fire, deep in conversation with Lisa Templeton. She hadn't seen them together throughout most of the evening, but the boldness of Lisa's earlier remark left Deirdre curiously doubtful of the woman.

Those doubts increased when Garth suddenly threw back his head and laughed over something Lisa had said. Deirdre dragged her eyes away from the couple, but found she could no longer concentrate on the conversation around her. She excused herself and quietly slipped away.

I have no reason to be jealous, Deirdre told herself as she poured more wine into her glass. Garth was the sort of man who would always attract beautiful women. Beautiful! When did Lisa Templeton get promoted from pretty to beautiful? Oh, God, Deirdre thought, bringing a hand to her temple. This is crazy. I can't go on living this way. I can't let thoughts of Garth take over my life.

"Having a good time?" Garth asked, walking up quietly behind her.

Deirdre spun around and nearly stumbled into his arms. He reached out to help her, but she pulled away quickly. Harsh lines appeared instantly around his mouth.

"It's a nice party," she said, feeling foolish for her reaction. She forced herself to stand quite still.

"Yes, I guess it must be, considering the amount of wine you've consumed."

Deirdre's eyes widened. "Have you been counting?" she asked.

"Just looking out for you, darling. What's the matter? Isn't Roy's attentiveness working its magic on you this evening?"

Deirdre lifted her glass and took a sip of the wine. If Garth had been as observant as he claimed, he'd know she had been nursing her second glass since dinner and had simply added more to it.

"If Roy bothers you, why did you invite him?" she asked, studying him with challenging eyes.

A sharp brow lifted and a distinct smile played at the corners of his mouth. "I didn't invite him. I assumed you had."

"Me! Roy said he called this afternoon and you . . ." She paused, remembering the pleased look on Craig's face when he noticed the confrontation between Roy and Garth. "Roy must have meant Craig." How typical of the old Craig to pull such a stunt. Bring the contenders together and may the best man win. Instinctively she knew his money was on Garth. Maybe Craig thought he was helping, by making her realize just who the better man was. As if she needed any help, she mused.

"What were the two of you talking about earlier?" she asked, circling the rim of her wineglass with her finger.

"You, of course," said Garth, taking the glass from her

and drinking from it. He made a face. "Craig's taste in wine leaves much to be desired." Deirdre laughed agreeably, and Garth went on. "Roy felt it was his duty to explain about the two of you being together last night."

Deirdre arched a brow. "And that made you angry?"

The moonlight reflected the gleam in his eye. "If you must know, I didn't like the way he presented his case. Apparently he wants his divorce very badly, but not if he has to pay for it. He's afraid that if Olivia gets the idea there's another woman in the picture, she might get very greedy."

Deirdre frowned in distaste. "I already told you Roy and I are not involved. Perhaps you misunderstood his reasons for telling you about last night."

Garth smiled sardonically. "Believe me, darling, I understood perfectly. Roy wants his divorce and he wants you, both on his terms. He suggested I might want to obtain a quiet divorce outside the country. It would be less embarrassing for everyone involved."

Deirdre had no reason to doubt his word; she was merely surprised by his honesty. "What did you tell him?" she couldn't resist asking. Roy had gone too far and she would handle him in due time, but, for now, she needed very much to hear what Garth had told him.

It seemed an eternity before he answered. When he did, he lifted a hand and touched her throat gently, saying, "I didn't tell him anything, Deirdre. This is between you and me only. Last night I wanted you desperately. My only regret is that I let my insane jealousy spoil what should have been very beautiful between us. If I had waited, I would have known instinctively that you had never been with Roy . . . or any other man. And you must know I've never felt that way about Jasamin or any other woman since that day I met you."

"How could I know that?" she asked, afraid her voice would betray her innermost feelings. She knew she could never settle for the kind of marriage he was offering, and the knowledge was tearing her apart inside. But she could never accept it—not for herself or for her son. Andy needed more from a father and God knew she needed so much more from a husband.

His fingers gently massaged her neck. "The same way that I know, my love. Because I love you and all the passion in me belongs only to you. I've never forgotten the passionate creature I made love to so long ago. You came alive in my arms, Deirdre. You were totally uninhibited when we made love. You are a woman fully aware of her own sexuality—her needs and desires. The only way you could have remained faithful to me all these years is if you love me, too."

Her breathing became erratic but Deirdre knew she couldn't control it unless she got away from Garth. His nearness was becoming intoxicating, his voice compelling, and she knew that any second now she'd be clinging to him, surrendering to the dictates of her heart and ignoring the dictates of her mind.

"It's not enough!" Deirdre cried, feeling the tears swimming in her eyes. "Damnit, it's not enough!"

Only with great effort did Deirdre keep herself from running into the house, regardless of the guests. Miraculously she retained her composure, but she was grateful the party was beginning to break up. When she returned from seeing the Gleasons off with Craig, she found an uncomfortable Jasamin cornered by Roy. Deirdre joined the conversation to see if she could help the girl out.

"Your plans seem rather vague, Jasamin. I imagine you'll be leaving when Garth does."

"I guess that will depend on Garth," Jasamin replied, neatly evading Roy's maneuvers while darting a quick look at Deirdre.

Roy shifted his feet uncomfortably. "I can't see Garth wanting to stay here for any length of time. His life is there, after all. It's probably the only place he'd really be happy."

Jasamin bit her lip. "I wouldn't know. If you're so curious, why don't you ask Garth?"

Roy drew a deep breath and looked uneasily at Deirdre. "Garth has been very evasive about his plans, Jasamin. I thought perhaps you could clarify them for me. You are his secretary, after all."

"His *business* secretary. He doesn't confide in me as far as personal matters are concerned, and, frankly, I don't think it's any of your business, either. Now, if you'll excuse me, I think I'll say good night."

Roy smoldered silently for several moments after she'd left. "Why don't I walk you to your car, Roy," Deirdre suggested, taking his arm and forcing him to comply.

"That girl is as slick as he is," Roy declared hotly as they walked toward the drive. Deirdre laughed softly.

"Why don't you just give up, Roy? Garth isn't going to tell you his plans until he's ready."

Roy frowned. "You deserve some answers, Deirdre. He has no right to keep you in suspense this way."

"I'm hardly in suspense," she said derisively. "Go home, Roy, and get a good night's sleep. We'll discuss those tax papers tomorrow."

Roy climbed into his car. "I'll call you," he promised, and then muttered as he put the key into the ignition, "God, I'll be glad when he's gone again!"

Gone again. Those words echoed in Deirdre's mind long after she had returned to her room, after accepting Jasamin and Craig's offer to clean up. She showered, washed her hair, and dried it slowly, knowing that if she went to bed, she'd only lie awake thinking about Garth.

Staring into the mirror, she realized that the woman she saw reflected there was different from the one she'd known before Garth returned. Her features were feminine yet strong, young yet worldly. And she was very much in love.

Either make a commitment or break it off entirely, the voice reminded her. But now those words sounded insignificant. Divorce wasn't the answer. She couldn't stop loving him simply because he was no longer her husband.

Deirdre buried her face in her hands and cried softly.

Her future might be uncertain, but she could no longer take for granted what she had in the present. She had to make the time with him count for something.

Deirdre pulled on her pink satin robe and tied the sash at her waist. In the hallway, she heard music and the sound of Jasamin's and Craig's laughter coming from the living room.

The light shone beneath the door of Garth's room and Deirdre walked toward it just as she had the night before. But this time she didn't knock before she turned the handle and went in.

Again, the room was empty, but she heard the water running in the shower. Deirdre turned out the lights and opened the French windows. She stepped out onto the balcony, hoping the crisp night air would help clear her head. You could be making a terrible mistake, she told herself. And yet, she knew leaving Garth's room was impossible.

She heard the bathroom door open. Her chance for escape, even if she'd wanted one, was gone.

From the balcony Deirdre could see him silhouetted by the bathroom light behind him. He paused for a moment, as if puzzled by the darkened room, and then he turned toward the partly opened balcony doors. For a moment he just stood there, and then, as if realizing it must be her, he crossed the room in long strides.

"Deirdre, for God's sake, what are you doing out there?" He stepped out and his hands gripped her arms. "My God, you're freezing! Come back inside," he ordered, leading her back into the room and shutting the doors tightly behind them.

When he turned back to her, Deirdre enfolded herself in his unsuspecting arms. "Don't talk, Garth. Just love me," she whispered. "Please, just for tonight."

"Deirdre," he breathed against her hair as his hands slid over the satin fabric covering her back.

Deirdre's hands touched the bare flesh at his throat, but

she curled them into balls when she slipped them inside his robe. "My hands are cold. I'm sorry."

Garth breathed deeply as he lifted her face to his. "Then warm them against me, my darling. I've been waiting so long for this moment, I hadn't even noticed."

His head bent and with a feathery softness, his mouth met hers. The pressure of his kiss deepened with his mounting passion and Garth drew her to him, molding her to the hard length of his body.

"Oh, God, I love you so much," he whispered against her lips, parting them with his tongue in his eagerness to explore the sweetened depths he knew she possessed. "I was right, wasn't I, Deirdre? You do love me, too."

"Oh, yes, I love you. I've always loved you, even though I tried so hard not to."

The robe slid easily from her shoulders and fell to the ground. She wore a nightgown made of a wispy fabric and Garth seemed unsure of how to handle it. He got as far as sliding the straps from her shoulders before saying, "You'd better do this before I tear it."

Deirdre laughed softly. "I wouldn't care if you did tear it," she said as she eased the gown over her head.

"I'll buy you hundreds more, my love," Garth said, examining her naked beauty with evident pleasure. His hand cupped her full breast. "On second thought, I won't buy you any. I don't want anything between us. Not even a scrap of material."

Deirdre smiled. "Then get rid of that thing," she ordered playfully, tugging at the sash of his robe. She purred, discovering his nakedness beneath. "Don't you ever sleep in anything?" she asked, pressing her body close to his.

"No," he whispered, bending his head to hers. "And I never get cold. I have the memory of you to keep me warm," he confessed, claiming her lips in a fiery embrace.

Deirdre laced her arms tightly around his neck, fighting back the tears his words had brought. If she was to have only memories, then she would savor them, each and every one.

"I love you," Deirdre whispered, breathless from the kiss. She lowered her mouth to press a kiss to the hollow of his throat. "Take me to bed, Garth, and hold me close."

Garth carried her to the bed and lay down beside her. He drew the covers over them and cradled Deirdre in his arms, content just to hold her, as she had asked.

After a while he said, "You've fulfilled my fantasy, darling. You'll never know how many nights I've dreamed of you coming to me this way, giving yourself freely, letting me love you the way I've always known I could."

"The way it was the first time?" she asked, spreading her fingers over the soft, damp curls of hair on his chest.

"No, darling. Better. Infinitely better."

Deirdre rose on one elbow and looked down at him. The light from the bath was still on and she was glad. In the half-light, he looked like a piece of Greek sculpture. He was truly a beautiful man, who was very touchable. She slid her hand daringly down the path the arrow of his hair made on his body.

"Are you accustomed to making such promises, darling?" she asked, knowing he wouldn't misunderstand her. "Because if you aren't, you'd better think about retracting that statement. But if you insist on proving it, I shall have to insist on guaranteed satisfaction—you'll have to keep doing it until this customer is satisfied."

Garth laughed huskily, then moaned pleasurably when her fingers spread over the flatness of his stomach. "How do I know you won't lie and say you're not satisfied when you really are?"

Deirdre bent her smooth, silken thigh over the roughened hair of his leg. "Oh, I think you'll know if I'm lying or not."

Garth moaned again, more urgently this time. "If you don't stop that, we're not going to have a chance to find out if *you're* lying. Remember, darling, it's been a long time since I've held the woman who drives me wild in my arms."

Her hand stopped its motion and came to rest on his inner thigh. "Last night wasn't such a long time ago," she reminded him playfully.

Garth changed positions with her swiftly, kicking the covers aside in the process. "Last night we took from each other without giving. I don't intend to ever let that happen again."

Deirdre lifted her hands to his face, the teasing playfulness vanishing swiftly from her eyes. "Neither do I, Garth. I promise you that."

Slowly Garth began to feed the fire within her. It was all so clear to her now. Lit on the night of their first union, that fire had never gone out. The denial of the past four years had been a sham. She hadn't let herself think consciously of that night because she feared the loneliness such thoughts would cause. But those memories had been there all the same. Now she realized that if she had allowed Garth to leave again without experiencing his extraordinary lovemaking, she wouldn't have survived.

The fire burned deep inside her, mounting slowly. Garth seemed to touch the core of it as he pressed kisses to her stomach and thighs, while his hands explored the provocative curves of her body.

Deirdre bent a thigh against him, eliciting a groan of sweet desire from him that momentarily drove them both beyond control. His mouth came back to hers, kissing her heatedly as he moved onto her, seeking passage into her body and soul.

Pulses telegraphed to her brain, at first slowly and rhythmically but finally in a crescendo that drove Deirdre beyond control of her own thoughts, her own cries. At some point she ceased to be a vessel receiving or giving pleasure. She became a part of him and her arms encircled him as though they were encircling herself.

"Together, my love," said Garth, sinking heavily against her, "together all the way." His words hit Deirdre with demanding, pulsating force, shooting spasms of sheer ecstasy through her body.

His gentle voice whispered to her now, murmuring words of love that affected her as profoundly as the love-making itself. What a glorious way to descend, caught up in this whirlpool of words and heartfelt emotions. She felt the vibrations in her own throat as she repeated those words like an echo.

"You're mine, my love. Totally, completely mine," Garth murmured, drawing her into the cradle of his arms as he rolled his weight from her.

"I've always been yours, darling. Please, please believe that. I never wanted to be free of you. I could never be, even if I had wanted to. My heart will never let go."

Garth kissed her temple, then left her long enough to draw the covers over them again. Lying beside her, he said, "I take it the customer is satisfied?"

"Mmm," she purred, snuggling close to him, as close as was humanly possible. "But I'll take a warranty just in case."

Garth laughed huskily, then murmured quietly, "A warranty for a lifetime. I'll see that the papers are drawn up tomorrow."

Chapter Twelve

The sky was overcast the next morning when Deirdre awoke. Only the realization that she was alone in the huge bed kept her from wanting to stay there. She would have willingly forgotten that Saturday was the busiest day of the work week if Garth had been beside her. As far as she was concerned, their lovemaking should go on forever; it was the only way to keep the world at bay. Although Deirdre admitted the selfishness of her mood, she longed for the oblivion she found in Garth's arms.

She left the bed and went back to her own room, where she showered and prepared for the day. The spray of water drove the lethargy from her body but along with greater alertness came thoughts she knew she had to face sooner or later. She couldn't just go through each day as if tomorrow would never come. She had to face Garth's leaving and, somehow, she had to help Andy face it as well. Tomorrow was Sunday. She would plan a special day, just for the three of them, and they would talk about it openly. They would make the most of their time together, even if the parting killed her.

Walking past the open doorway of Jasamin's room, Deirdre couldn't help but glance in. When she found her packing, Deirdre stopped short and tapped on the doorframe.

"Jasamin, is something wrong?" she asked when the girl glanced up with tear-reddened eyes.

"Oh . . . no, no. Nothing is wrong." She looked away hastily. "I've just decided to make that trip to New York today. I really shouldn't have come here anyway," she admitted ruefully. "I don't know what I thought I could accomplish."

"You mean with Craig." When Jasamin nodded, Deirdre added, "I'm sorry it didn't work out. Perhaps it's just too soon, Jasamin. Craig was bitter for so long and, from what you've told me, I know it was because he loved you very deeply." She paused, her heart going out to the girl. "I honestly thought when you told him about your . . . well, about your breakdown after the accident . . ."

"I didn't tell him," said Jasamin weakly, closing the lid of her suitcase. Deirdre looked incredulous. "I thought I could last night, but the words wouldn't come. You see, Deirdre, I realized last night that if I let myself, I could fall in love with Craig. But I'm nothing more to him than a proving ground. If he could face me without bitterness, then he could go on with his life and never look back. I'm happy for him, Deirdre. Truly I am. But I also feel very vulnerable right now and if I don't go away, I'm afraid of what might happen."

Deirdre leaned weakly against the door frame. "Does Garth know you plan to leave today?"

Jasamin shook her head. "I didn't get a chance to tell him before he left this morning. I'll try to reach him in Washington, but if not, he'll know where he can find me."

Deirdre felt her stomach tighten as if she were going to be ill. "Garth drove to Washington this morning?"

"Yes, didn't he tell you?" Jasamin looked confused. "Oh, well, maybe he wanted to wait and tell you his plans once he got everything settled. His leave of absence is almost up and I'm sure he has arrangements to make."

"Yes, I'm sure he does," Deirdre agreed. "He's probably anxious to get back to work." So much for being brave and strong, she thought, wishing she could be alone now simply to cry her eyes out. "Will you be joining him, Jasamin?"

Suddenly, Jasamin's blue eyes widened in surprise, as she stared beyond Deirdre to where Craig had appeared.

How much of their conversation he had overheard Deirdre couldn't guess. If his expression was anything to go by, she guessed he hadn't missed much.

"Last night you didn't mention anything about leaving," Craig said woodenly.

Jasamin looked uncomfortable as Deirdre moved aside to let Craig into the room. "I . . . didn't think it was worth mentioning," the young girl stammered.

"Oh, didn't you!" Craig exclaimed tersely.

Deirdre knew when her presence wasn't needed or wanted. But as she turned to leave the two alone Craig laid her worst fears to rest. The words he spoke to Jasamin proved, as nothing else could, that he was well on the way to a full recovery.

In a gruff voice Craig whispered to Jasamin, "Please, don't go. I heard what you said, Jasamin, and it just isn't so—you're much more than a proving ground to me. Please stay. I know we can work things out if we try."

Deirdre heard no more, but she didn't need to.

She went downstairs and had breakfast with Edith and Andy. Edith asked if she could take Andy to her grandson's birthday party later that morning and, as the idea thrilled Andy, Deirdre agreed readily and left for work.

Just after ten, Roy paid her a surprise visit. He walked straight into her small office and ordered Sally from the room.

"It's all right, Sally," Deirdre assured her, knowing the girl wasn't oblivious of the anger emanating from Roy.

"I'll be right outside," Sally promised, shooting Roy a warning look.

"Oh, good God!" Roy groaned, but his words bounced off the closed door. "You'd think I was planning to murder you!"

Deirdre rose from the desk, where she'd been preparing the bank deposit. "You do look rather angry," she said with a smile.

"And why shouldn't I be? Your husband paid me a

visit at my place first thing this morning," he informed her. "After all we've been through together, Deirdre, don't you think I deserved to hear it from you?"

Her eyes widened. "I'm sorry, Roy. I didn't know Garth planned to see you this morning."

He took a step back, reconsidering his accusation. "Then it's not true? You and he aren't sleeping together?"

Her mouth gaped at his blatant question. "Did Garth tell you that?"

Roy drew a sharp breath. "He told me. Perhaps not like that, but the message was clear. He has no intention of letting you go, Deirdre."

Deirdre lowered her eyes. "I never asked him to, Roy."

Roy sighed heavily. "I can't believe you would willingly commit yourself to the kind of life he's offering you. You're married to him only because of Andy."

Deirdre stiffened noticeably. No matter what anyone thought, conceiving her lover's child had never been a source of shame for Deirdre and she wasn't about to start defending herself now.

"I can't expect you to understand, Roy. But I do want you to know that I value your friendship and I wouldn't want to lose it. In spite of everything, I think Garth feels the same way. The two of you were friends for a very long time," she reminded him.

Roy arched a brow. "Is that why he told me my services were no longer needed and to stay the hell away from you?"

Deirdre gasped. "He told you that?"

Roy nodded. "He also demanded to see the file I've been keeping on you."

"The file!" Deirdre exclaimed. She knew it existed, of course, but why Garth would demand access to it now was beyond her. Did he plan to hire another attorney to replace Roy? "Did you let him see it?" she asked.

"He didn't give me much choice," Roy sneered. "He would have torn my office apart looking for it. God only knows what he wanted with it, but he's got it now. Just like he's got you."

Deirdre bit her lip. "He's my husband, Roy. I can't even think about being free of him. Even if it means I'll have to live without him for months at a time, at least we'll have moments together like the few we've shared."

Roy closed his eyes. "I guess I've made a prize fool of myself, haven't I?"

Deirdre reached out and took his hands. "Not to me. You've seen me through the hardest times of my life, and I'll never be able to thank you enough. Please try to understand, Roy. I care too much about you to pretend we can ever be more than just friends."

For a long while Roy did nothing but stare at her. Then, suddenly, as if having made a decision, he released her hands and reached into the inside pocket of his jacket and withdrew an envelope. As he handed it to her Deirdre saw her name scrawled on the outside. The envelope was open.

She looked up at him as he said, "You might not believe this, but until Garth demanded access to your file this morning, I forgot all about having this. I know now I made a mistake in not giving it to you before, but if you think back to the way you felt at the time, you might find it in your heart to forgive me."

He left her then. Deirdre stared long and hard at the envelope in her hands. Taking out the letter, she sat down and read it.

> Deirdre:
>
> I've just seen our son for the first time and I can't tell you what it meant to me. I want so much to come to you, darling. To share this time with you and to let you know how deeply I care for you. But I know I can't. Roy has explained how difficult these past months have been for you, and I know that with Craig just out of the hospital himself, my presence will only make things more difficult for the two of you. The timing always

seems to be wrong for us, Deirdre, but I know the day will come when I'll be able to come to you so that we can begin our life together, with nothing standing between us. Until then I'll hold the picture of our newborn son in my heart, just as I have the memory of the night we spent together.

GARTH

Deirdre stared at the letter until the tears she shed made the ink run. She raged with anger at Roy, but she also understood that he had believed he'd done the right thing in keeping the letter from her.

Not once in all those years had Deirdre considered how Garth felt at being kept from his child. But, then, she'd never had any reason to believe he cared for her or ever really wanted the baby. This letter would have proved how wrong she had been. It could have changed everything.

Sally and Debbie both camc toward her when she emerged from the office a few minutes later. "I'm going home for the day. Can you two manage by yourselves?"

They exchanged a look. "Surc, Deirdre," said Sally. Touching her arm lightly, she added, "Are you all right?"

Deirdre assured her that she was and left the store, anxious to be home when Garth rcturned. She was certain he would, if only to say good-bye.

The house was empty when she got there. She assumed Edith had taken Andy to her daughter's house, and a quick glance out the window told her Craig had taken the *Jessy Bess* for a sail.

Changing into a pair of jeans, Deirdre walked down to the dock and climbed aboard the sloop. She took her time looking around as she began to realize why Garth had bought the boat. He had been establishing a foothold in her life any way he could, and she thrilled to the knowledge of this gesture. She would welcome him into her life for as much time as he could give her, "until nothing stands between us." Not even his job.

Deirdre was exploring the cabin area, imagining the trips she and Garth would one day take in the boat, when she heard footsteps on the deck. She came up from the cabin just as Garth was about to come down, and he smiled at the sight of her.

"I was hoping I'd find you here. I must have just missed you at the store."

Deirdre extended a hand and allowed him to pull her from the cabin area. "You've had a busy morning," she said, enfolding herself in his arms and receiving his kiss before leading the way off the boat. Once they reached the dock their arms went around each other's waist and they walked back toward the house.

"I had some business to take care of," he admitted, clearing his throat. "I planned on being back in time to take you to lunch."

"Oh, really! In that case we can have lunch here. We could take the boat out and have a picnic, since it's such a lovely day. Or we could have lunch here, since we have the house all to ourselves," she added slyly.

Garth stopped short and drew her into his arms. "Come to think of it, I'm not all that hungry. Let's spend the afternoon making love instead."

Deirdre laughed. "You missed your chance this morning. I just love staying in bed on overcast mornings. Besides, I'm starving."

Garth lowered his mouth to hers and spoke softly against her lips. "We'll compromise and have lunch in bed."

The idea was tempting and Deirdre agreed readily. In the kitchen she found a note from Craig tacked to the message board: "Have taken Jasamin to the cabin for a few days. Need time to sort things out. Craig."

Deirdre passed the note to Garth, who read it and smiled. "I wouldn't be listening for any wedding bells right away if I were you."

"Darling, I may be a hopeless romantic in some ways, but I'm not totally naive."

"Mmmm, perhaps not. But as I recall, that cabin has a powerful aura about it that even the stoniest heart can't ignore."

"You mean like yours?" Deirdre teased, lifting a hand to stroke his cheek.

"I'll admit I gave it a noble fight."

"Yes, I remember. Are you sorry?"

Garth looked surprised at her question. "I'm sorry for a lot of things in my life, Deirdre, but making love with you that night and making you pregnant is not one of them. Perhaps I should be. Perhaps it's selfish of me, knowing how much you've had to endure alone."

"It was . . . difficult," she admitted.

His brow creased sharply. "You had only to send for me, Deirdre. Last night you claimed you've always loved me, but you never let me know. For years now I've been thinking about how much you must hate me. I know it was hard for you, Deirdre, but I was willing to be here with you. Do you know what it was like for me, believing that you married me only because of Andy, and that you regretted what was the most beautiful night of my life?"

"I didn't know you cared about me or Andy until Roy came to see me this morning," she confessed. "I assumed, as you had, that you married me only because I carried your child. Garth, I had no reason to believe otherwise, until . . ." She paused and drew the letter from her pocket. "Roy showed me this just a little while ago."

Garth looked it over and she saw fire light his eyes as realization swept over him. "That bastard! I'll kill him!"

"Garth, please don't be angry with Roy!" she cried pleadingly. "He did what he thought was best at the time. I'd like to think things would have been different for us if I'd known how you felt, but I can't honestly say what I would have done if I'd seen this letter then. I'm not sure . . . I would have believed it," she confessed weakly. "Your work has always been so important to you, and if I thought you'd given it up just because I'd had your child, I don't think we could have ever had a real marriage."

Garth raked his hands through his hair. "What do you expect me to say now, Deirdre?" he asked harshly. "That I believe the things you told me last night . . . that you came to me because you love me and wanted to be with me?"

Deirdre shook her head in confusion. "I did," she breathed, wondering why he would doubt her. "What other reason would I have had? Oh, Garth, look at me!" she pleaded when he turned away from her. "Tell me why you think I came to you."

His eyes bore into hers. "You thought I was leaving you, didn't you, Deirdre? Did you convince yourself you should make the most of our time together?"

Deirdre swallowed hard. "I thought that's what you wanted."

Garth's eyes closed tightly. "Damn you for that," he groaned as he turned away completely. "So, Roy over-played his hand in thinking you would divorce me for him," he said, throwing back his head with a deep sigh. "But I wonder about the next man who comes along, Deirdre. How long will it be before you decide you want a full-time lover for yourself, and a full-time father for your son?"

Her eyes swam with tears. "If that's what you believe, I think it would be best if you left now. I came to you last night for one reason only: to show you that I loved you enough to accept the fact that I won't have you with me for several months out of the year. In spite of Andy's needs or mine, I was willing to accept you on your terms, no matter what the cost." She watched as Garth turned toward her. "You claim to know me better than I know myself, but you don't, Garth. You don't know me at all."

His hands came out but she slipped easily from his grasp and raced from the room. Reaching her room, Deirdre fell sobbing across the bed. Just as she realized she hadn't locked the door she heard it open.

"Go away, Garth. Please, just go away," she sobbed as

Garth's hands touched her shoulders, turning her over to draw her into his arms.

"Is that what you really want, Deirdre? Do you want me to leave for months at a time, and come home only to see you and Andy for occasional visits?"

Her arms moved of their own volition to lace tightly around his neck. "No," she sobbed breathlessly. "I'm sorry. I thought I could be stronger, but I can't bear the thought of your leaving again."

Garth pressed his warm lips to her tear-moistened cheek. "I want the words to come from you, Deirdre. You've never asked anything of me but to give our son my name, but now I need so much to hear you ask more of me. Say it, darling. Tell me you want me to stay."

She compressed her lips tightly. "I promised I wouldn't ask more than you felt you could give, but these last few days, it's been very hard to keep that promise. I want very much for you to stay, darling. But if you can't, I want you to know there will never be another man in my life, nor will there ever be another father for Andy. He needs you, Garth, and so do I. Please, Garth, find a way to be with us."

Garth drew a deep breath and lay her back on the bed, covering her body with his own. "I had planned on taking you to dinner tonight, so you could meet the people I had dinner with that first night you stayed at the hospital with Andy. They're Ted and Laura Ames, and, as of this morning, Ted is officially my new law partner."

Deirdre gasped. "You mean here!"

Garth laughed huskily. "Not exactly, darling. My specialty is federal law, and I'm afraid that means Washington, D.C. Of course, it also means living there through the week. But coming home on weekends is a lot more appealing than coming home a few weeks a year. Would you mind that terribly?"

The delight danced vividly in her eyes. "Only if we couldn't live there with you through the week. At least some of the time. I've got a business to run, remember?"

"I'm willing to compromise," murmured Garth, nuzzling her neck.

"As we did about having lunch in bed? I have a feeling your compromises will never be fifty-fifty."

Garth smiled, his eyes filled with happiness. "What can you expect from a man who loves you one hundred percent?"

RAPTURE ROMANCE

Coming next month

TENDER RHAPSODY

by Jennifer Dale

Unable to fulfill her dream of becoming a classical pianist, Judith Vanover had turned to musical agenting. But she kept her standards high, scorning popular musicians—until she met Oliver. Forced to accept the charismatic rock star as a client, she swore the relationship would go no further. But her heartbeat had already become the hard, driving rhythm of his rock-and-roll . . .

SUMMER STORM

by Joan Wolf

Chris was a struggling actor and Mary a scholar—still their marriage was a perfect, passionate union. But the glitter of Hollywood and a dazzling starlet stole Chris away. Then, in the flesh of reporters' cameras they met again. Had super-star Chris come to reestablish their marriage . . . or end it?

RAPTURE ROMANCE—*Reader's Opinion Questionnaire*

Thank you for filling out our questionnaire. Your response to the following questions will help us to bring you more and better books, by telling us what you are like, what you look for in a romance, and how we can best keep you informed about our books. Your opinions are important to us, and we appreciate your help.

1. What made you choose this particular book? (This book is #______)
   Art on the front cover______
   Plot descriptions on the back cover______
   Friend's recommendation______
   Other (please specify)________________________
2. Would you rate this book:
   Excellent______
   Very good______
   Good______
   Fair______
3. Were the love scenes (circle answers):
   A. Too explicit   Not explicit enough   Just right
   B. Too frequent   Not frequent enough   Just right
4. How many Rapture Romances have you read?______
5. Number, from most favorite to least favorite, romance lines you enjoy:
   Adventures in Love______
   Ballantine Love and Life______
   Bantam Circle of Love______
   Dell Candlelight ______
   Dell Candlelight Ecstasy______
   Jove Second Chance at Love______
   Harlequin______
   Harlequin Presents______
   Harlequin Super Romance______
   Rapture Romance______
   Silhouette______
   Silhouette Desire______
   Silhouette Special Edition______
6. Please check the *types* of romances you enjoy:
   Historical romance______
   Regency romance______
   Romantic suspense______
   Short, light contemporary romance______
   Short, sensual contemporary romance______
   Longer contemporary romance______
7. What is the age of the oldest ______ youngest ______ heroine you would like to read about? The oldest ______ youngest ______ hero?

8. What elements do you dislike in a romance?
   Mystery/suspense_____
   Supernatural_____
   Other (please specify) ______________________________
9. We would like to know:
   - How much television you watch
     Over 4 hours a day_____
     2–4 hours a day_____
     0–2 hours a day_____
   - What your favorite programs are
     ____
     ____
   - When you usually watch television
     8 a.m. to 5 p.m._____
     5 p.m. to 11 p.m._____
     11 p.m. to 2 a.m._____
10. How many magazines do you read regularly?
    More than 6_____
    3–6_____
    0–3_____
    Which of these are your favorites?
    ____
    ____

To get a picture of our readers, and to know where to reach them, the following personal information will be most helpful, if you don't mind giving it, and will be kept only for our records.

Name ______________________________
Address______________________________
City ______________________________
State__________ Zip code__________

Please check your age group:
   17 and under_____
   18–34_____
   35–49_____
   50–64_____
   64 and older_____

Education:
   Now in high school_____
   Now in college_____
   Graduated from high school_____
   Completed some college_____
   Graduated from college_____

Are you now working outside the home?
   Yes_____ No_____
   Full time_____
   Part time_____
   Job title_____

Thank you for your time and effort. Please send the completed questionnaire and answer sheet to: Robin Grunder, RAPTURE ROMANCE, New American Library, 1633 Broadway, New York, NY 10019